"What are you doing here?"

She grinned and tipped her head to the side. "Paul, I live here."

"I mean, why aren't you at the hospital?" He tried to ignore the rush of happiness that filled his chest.

"Sophie is doing better, and I needed to come home and get some things done. I've been wearing the same dress since we took Sophie to the hospital. It was time for a change."

"That's great. How are you?" She looked fine to him. Better than fine. She looked wonderful.

He studied her lovely face. A light blush colored her cheeks, and her eyes had dark circles under them but they sparkled now as she gazed at him. A soft smile curved her lips. She was happy to see him.

Clara wasn't his type, so why was he so delighted to see her?

After thirty-five years as a nurse, **Patricia Davids** hung up her stethoscope to become a full-time writer. She enjoys spending her free time visiting her grandchildren, doing some long-overdue yard work and traveling to research her story locations. She resides in Wichita, Kansas. Pat always enjoys hearing from her readers. You can visit her online at patriciadavids.com.

Books by Patricia Davids

Love Inspired

The Amish Bachelors

An Amish Harvest
An Amish Noel
His Amish Teacher
Their Pretend Amish Courtship
Amish Christmas Twins
An Unexpected Amish Romance
His New Amish Family

Lancaster Courtships

The Amish Midwife

Brides of Amish Country

Plain Admirer
Amish Christmas Joy
The Shepherd's Bride
The Amish Nanny
An Amish Family Christmas: A Plain Holiday
An Amish Christmas Journey
Amish Redemption

Visit the Author Profile page at Harlequin.com for more titles.

His New
Amish Family

Patricia Davids

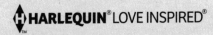

Recycling programs
for this product may
not exist in your area.

LOVE INSPIRED BOOKS

ISBN-13: 978-1-335-42816-5

His New Amish Family

Copyright © 2018 by Patricia MacDonald

www.Harlequin.com

Printed in U.S.A.

If any man among you seem to be religious, and bridleth not his tongue, but deceiveth his own heart, this man's religion is vain. Pure religion and undefiled before God and the Father is this, to visit the fatherless and widows in their affliction, and to keep himself unspotted from the world.

—*James* 1:26–27

This book is dedicated with love and respect to my daughter Kathy. Thanks for all your help and the two wonderful grandkids. Mama Loves You.

Chapter One

"This is what you spent our money on?"

"It's *wunderbar, ja*? What a beauty." Paul Bowman grinned as he wiped a spot of dirt off the white trailer bearing his name in large black letters on the side. It might look like a big white box with windows but it was his future. It sat parked inside their uncle's barn out of the weather.

His brother, Mark, shook his head. "Beauty was not my first thought."

Paul stepped back to take in the full effect. "Paul Bowman Auction Services. Has a nice sound, don't you think? A friend did all the custom work. He found this used concession stand trailer, stripped it to a shell, then installed the sliding glass windows on each side, rewired it for battery power as well as electricity, installed the speakers on the roof and customized the inside to fit my needs. It did smell like fried funnel cakes for a while but the new paint job took care of that."

Mark sighed heavily. "This is not what I was expecting."

Paul walked around pointing to the features he had insisted on having. "It is mounted on a flatbed trailer with two axles and radial tires for highway travel. The front hitch is convertible. It can be pulled by horses or by a truck if the auction is more than twenty miles away."

"What were you thinking?"

Paul didn't understand the disapproval in his older brother's voice. "I told you I needed a better sound system. People have to be able to hear the auctioneer."

Mark gestured toward the trailer. "I thought you wanted a new speaker. This thing looks like a cross between a moving van and the drive-up window at the Farley State Bank. It's huge. And white. Our buggies must be black."

"The bishop won't object to the color. It's not like it's sunflower yellow and it isn't truly a buggy. It's my place of business. It has everything I need."

"Everything except an auction to take it to."

"The work will start rolling in. You'll see." He pulled open the back door. "You have got to hear this sound system. These speakers are awesome. It all runs on battery power, or I can plug it in if there is electricity at the place where the auction is being held. The bishop allows the use of electricity in some businesses so he shouldn't object to this."

"You will have to okay it with him. It isn't plain."

"I'll see him soon. I'm not worried."

"And if he says *nee*, can you get your money back?"

"He won't." Paul stepped up into what was essentially an office on wheels.

The trailer was outfitted with two desk spaces, two chairs and a dozen storage bins of assorted sizes secured to the walls. Sliding windows on both sides opened to let him deal directly with customers and call the auction without leaving the comfort of his chair. A third window at the front with an open slot beneath it served as a windshield so he could drive a team of horses from inside.

The feeling of elation that it all belonged to him widened Paul's smile. Mark didn't understand how much this meant. No one in the family did. They thought being an auctioneer was his hobby and nothing more. Maybe that was his fault.

He was the joker in the family. He was good at pretending he didn't take anything too seriously. He was a fellow who liked a good joke even if the joke was on him. He enjoyed light flirtations but avoided serious relationships at all costs. Auctioneering was his one true love.

This trailer was the culmination of three years' work to fulfill his dream of becoming a full-time auctioneer.

Detaching the microphone from the clips that held it in place while the vehicle was in motion, he flipped a switch and began his auctioneer's chant. "I have two hundred, um two, two, who'll give me three hundred, um three, three, I see three. Now who'll give me a little more, four, four, do I hear four?"

He slid open the window and propped his elbows on the desktop as he looked down at Mark. "What do you think?"

"It's mighty fancy for a fellow who has only been a licensed auctioneer for a couple of months."

Paul wanted his brother to share his enthusiasm, not dampen it. "I completed the auctioneer's course and served my year of apprenticeship with Harold Yoder. He's one of the best in these parts. I have called twenty auctions under his supervision. I have earned my license, and I'm ready to be out on my own."

"There's a difference between going out on

your own and going out on a limb. How much did you spend on this?"

"Enough." All he had saved plus the money he had borrowed from Mark and a four-thousand-dollar loan from the bank on a short-term note. Paul kept that fact to himself. He didn't need a lecture from his always practical older brother. Sometimes life required a leap of faith.

It was true he had expected to be hired for several major auctions by the time his custom trailer was finished but he'd had only one small job so far. His commission had barely covered his expenses for that one. He'd been forced to borrow the money to pay the builder when his trailer was ready. No Amish fellow liked being in debt but sometimes a man's business required it. Paul closed the window, switched off the microphone and stepped out.

Mark shook his head. "I hope you know what you're doing."

Paul grinned. "I talk fast. That's the secret. You'll see. This is a *goot* investment. You'll get your money back soon."

"I hope so. I'll need it to pay for the new ovens we're putting in at the bakery. Have you told Onkel Isaac about this purchase?"

"Not yet. I hope he approves but I know this was the right decision for me even if he doesn't." They both walked out into the early morning sunshine.

"He will support your decision but if you fail at this business venture, don't look to him to bail you out. Or me. Lessons learned by failure are as valuable as lessons learned by success."

"I know. It's the Amish way." Paul had heard that many times in his life but it never meant as much as it meant now. When his loan came due in two months, the bank could repossess his van if he didn't have the money. He was starting to worry.

Maybe he could get an extension on his loan. His uncle did a lot of business at the bank but Paul's finances were what they would look at.

He crossed the farmyard with Mark and headed toward their uncle's furniture-making business, where they both worked. As they entered the quiet shop, they went their separate ways. Mark went out back to start the diesel generator that produced the electric power for the numerous woodworking machines, lights and office equipment. When Paul heard the hum of the generator start up and the lights came on, he raised the large door at the rear of the building so the forklift operator could bring in pallets of raw wood and move finished products to the trucks that would soon arrive for the day's deliveries.

He saw a car turn into the parking lot and stop but he knew Mark would be up front soon to deal with any customers. A man got out of the car and walked toward Paul instead of going to the entrance to the business. He was dressed in khaki pants and a blue polo shirt. Definitely not an Amish fellow.

"I'm looking for the Amish auctioneer?"

Paul grinned and clapped a hand to his chest. "You found him. I'm Paul Bowman."

"I'm Ralph Hobson. I recently inherited a farm and I am no farmer. The place is a pile of rocks and weedy fields fit for goats and not much else. I've been told that an auction is the easiest and fastest way to get rid of the property."

"Auctions are very popular in this part of the country. The buyer can see he's getting a fair deal because he knows what everyone else is offering. The seller gets his money right away, and my auction service takes care of the details in between for a ten percent commission. Does that sound like something you're interested in?"

"It does. How soon can you hold an auction?"

"That depends on the size and condition of the property and the contents of the home if you are selling that."

"I am. The farm is a hundred and fifty-five acres. How much can I expect to get for it?"

"Farmland in this part of Ohio sells for between five and six thousand dollars an acre depending on the quality of the land."

Ralph's eyes lit up. "It's a good thing I didn't take the first offer I had. That weasel was trying to cheat me. So roughly seven hundred and seventy thousand, give or take a few thousand?"

Paul wondered who the weasel was and how much he had offered. It wasn't any of his business so he didn't ask. "Minus my commission. It could go higher if there is a bidding war."

"What's that?"

"That's when two or more bidders keep upping their bids because they both really want the item."

"That sounds interesting. What keeps the seller from putting someone in the crowd to drive the price up?" Ralph slipped his hands into the front pockets of his pants. "Hypothetically, of course."

"I won't say it never happens but the bidder is taking a chance he could get stuck with a high-priced item he doesn't want or can't afford if the other bidder quits first."

"I see." Ralph smiled but it didn't reach his eyes. "I guess we can both hope for a bidding war since you earn more if I make more. Right?"

"Right. Are there outbuildings? Farm equipment? Livestock? I'll need to make an accurate inventory of everything."

"A few chickens, three buggy horses and a cow with a calf are the only livestock. A neighbor has them for now. The rest is a lot of junk. My uncle rarely let go of anything."

Paul tried not to get his hopes up. "One man's junk is another man's treasure. I'll need to look the place over."

"I can drive you there now."

This was too good an opportunity to pass up. To handle an entire farm and household sale could bring him a hefty commission. Enough to pay back Mark and the bank loan plus get his business off to a good start. "Who owned the farm before you?"

"My uncle, Eli King."

"I think I know the place. Out on Cedar Road just after the turn off to Middleton?"

"That's right."

Paul had gone there last year with his cousin Luke looking for parts to fix an ancient washing machine. Ralph was right about his uncle collecting things but not all of it was junk. There were some valuable items stashed away. "Let me tell my uncle where I'm going and I'll be right with you."

"Great." The man looked relieved and walked back to his car.

Paul found his uncle, his cousin Samuel and Mark all conferring in the front office. Paul tipped his head toward the parking lot. "That *Englisch* fellow wants to show me a farm he plans to put up for auction. Can you spare me for a few hours?"

The men looked up from reviewing the day's work schedule. "Can we?" Isaac asked.

Samuel flipped to the last page on the clipboard he held. "It's not like he does much work when he is here."

Mark and Isaac chuckled. Paul smiled, too, not offended in the least. "Very funny, cousin. I do twice the amount of work my brother does these days. Mark spends more time at the bakery than he does here."

Mark's grin turned to a frown. Isaac patted his shoulder. "That is to be expected when he and his new wife are getting their own business up and running."

"That's right," Mark said, looking mollified. "It takes a lot of thought to decide which type of ovens we need and where they should be placed, what kind of storage we need—a hundred decisions have to be made."

Isaac's wife, Anna, ran a small gift shop across the parking lot from the woodworking building. Mark's wife, Helen, had been selling her baked goods in the shop and at local farmers markets but the increasing demand for her tasty treats and breads made opening a bakery the next logical step for them.

A month ago, the church community held a frolic to help Mark and Helen finish building their bakery next to the gift shop. The couple would live above the bakery until they could afford to build a new home. They were currently living with Helen's aunt, Charlotte Zook, but her home was several miles away, making it impractical to stay there once their business was up and running.

"When is the grand opening?" Isaac asked.

"The dual ovens we want are back-ordered. We can't set a date until they are paid for and installed." Mark gave Paul a pointed look. It was a reminder that he needed his money back soon.

Paul winked at his brother. "Mark's interest isn't in the new ovens. Sneaking a kiss from his new bride is what keeps him running over there."

Mark blushed bright red and everyone laughed.

Paul turned to Isaac for an answer. "Can you spare me today? I'm trying to get my own business up and running, too."

Isaac nodded. "We will do without you. Any idea when you'll be back?"

"I can't say for sure." He opened the door and saw his cousin Joshua and Joshua's wife, Mary, coming across from the gift shop. Mary carried her infant son balanced on her hip. The happy, chubby boy was trying to catch the ribbon of her *kapp* with one hand and stuff it in his mouth with little success.

Mary called out, "*Guder mariye*, Paul. Is Samuel around?"

"Good morning, Mary. He's inside."

"*Goot*, I need to speak to him. Don't forget about Nicky's birthday party two weeks from Saturday. You can bring a date if you like."

"I won't forget and I won't bring a date. Meet the family. Bounce the cute baby. That would be a sure way to give a woman the wrong impression," he called over his shoulder.

"You can't stay single forever," Mary shouted after him.

"I can try." He hurried toward Ralph Hobson's car. He didn't want to keep a potentially profitable client waiting.

On the twenty-minute ride, Paul did all the talking as he outlined the details of the auction contract and his responsibilities, including advertising and inventory, sorting the goods and cleaning up after the sale. Hobson listened and didn't say much.

Paul hoped the man understood what he was

agreeing to. "I'll send you a printed copy of all I've told you if you agree to hire me. A handshake will be enough to seal the deal."

"Fine, fine. Whatever." The man took one hand off the wheel and held it out.

Paul shook it. He was hired. It was hard to contain his joy and keep the smile off his face.

When Ralph turned into the lane of a neat Amish farmyard, Paul noticed a white car parked off to the side of the drive. Ralph stopped beside it. A middle-aged man in a white cowboy hat got out. He tossed a cigarette butt to the ground and came around to the driver's side. Ralph rolled down his window.

"Good morning, sir. My name is Jeffrey Jones. Are you the owner of this property?"

"I am," Ralph said.

"I understand this farm is for sale. I'd like to take a look at the property and maybe make an offer on it."

Ralph frowned. "Where did you hear it was for sale?"

The man shrugged and smiled. "Word gets around in a small community like this."

Ralph shook his head. "Your information isn't quite accurate. There will be a farm auction in the near future."

"Ah, that's a risky way to get rid of the place.

You should at least hear my offer. You've got no guarantee that an auction will top it."

"I'll take my chances," Ralph said. "Keep an eye out for the date of the sale. You might get it for less."

Mr. Jones stepped back from the vehicle. "Do the mineral rights go with the farmland or are they separate?"

"I'm not selling the mineral rights."

"Smart man. I imagine leasing those rights to the local coal mine will bring you a tidy sum for many years. My offer for the farm expires when I get in my car. No one is going to want this place except maybe a poor Amish farmer. You'll have trouble getting a decent price."

If Ralph sold the land now, Paul wouldn't get a dime but he had to put his client's interest before his own. "You should at least hear what the man had to offer."

"I have my heart set on an auction. Besides, I thought we had a deal. We shook on it."

Paul grinned. It seemed his new client was an honorable man. "It's up to you but he is mistaken if he thinks all Amish farmers are poor. You'll get a fair price at auction. You can put a reserve on it if you want. If the bidding doesn't reach your set price, it's a 'no sale' and you are free to sell it another way."

Ralph smiled. "I'm going to hope for a bidding war."

Mr. Jones appeared more puzzled than disappointed but he got back in his car and drove away.

Paul leaned forward in his seat to get a good look at the farm as they drove up. Both the barn and the house were painted white and appeared in good condition. He made a quick mental appraisal of the equipment he saw, then jotted down numbers in a small notebook he kept in his pocket.

"What is she doing here?" The anger in Ralph's voice shocked Paul.

He followed Ralph's line of sight and spied an Amish woman sitting on a suitcase on the front porch of the house. She wore a simple pale blue dress with an apron of matching material and a black cape thrown back over her shoulders. Her wide-brimmed black traveling bonnet hid her hair. She looked hot, dusty and tired. She held a girl of about three or four on her lap. The child clung tightly to her mother. A boy a few years older leaned against the door behind her holding a large calico cat.

"Who is she?" Paul asked.

"That is my annoying cousin Clara Fisher." Ralph opened his car door and got out. Paul did the same.

The woman glared at both men. "Why are there padlocks on the doors, Ralph? Eli never locked his home."

"They are there to keep unwanted visitors out. What are you doing here?" Ralph demanded.

"I live here. May I have the keys, please? My children and I are weary."

Ralph's eyebrows snapped together in a fierce frown. "What do you mean you live here?"

"What part did you fail to understand, Ralph? I…live…here," she said slowly, as if speaking to a small child.

Ralph's face darkened with anger. Paul had to turn away to keep from laughing.

"You can poke fun at me if you want but that is not an explanation." The man was livid.

Clara sat where she was, seemingly unruffled by his ire. "Eli invited us to live with him last Christmas. We moved in six months ago."

"No one told me that. I didn't see you at the funeral."

"We have been in Maryland visiting my mother for the past month." She stroked her little girl's hair. "Sophie became ill and was in the hospital briefly. Eli's friend Dan Kauffman called me to tell me about Eli's passing. He knew Mother and I couldn't return for the funeral. Surely he told you that, for I know he attended."

"I don't speak to the Amish and they don't speak to me. You'll have to find somewhere else to live. Uncle Eli left the farm to me."

Her eyes widened with astonishment. "I don't believe it. He told me he had amended the farm trust and made me the beneficiary months ago."

Ralph looked stunned but he quickly recovered and glared at her. "Even if he did, he revoked that amendment three weeks ago when he made me the new trustee. He said nothing about you or your children. That's why they call it a revocable trust, Clara, because a man can change his mind anytime. It's irrevocable now that Eli is gone and this farm belongs to me."

Paul wished he knew more about how such things worked.

"You're lying, Ralph. Eli wouldn't turn over his farm to you."

"You make it sound like we weren't on speaking terms. I came to visit the old fellow at least once a year."

"Only to see if you could beg money off him."

"I admit my motives weren't always the best but things have been different lately. I cared about the old guy."

"Cared about what you could get from him. Open the door at once."

Ralph crossed his arms and leaned back. "You haven't changed, cousin. You're still trying to boss me around. I'm not going to let you in my house."

"You *have* changed. You've gone from scamming Amish folks out of a few hundred dollars to stealing costlier things, like this farm."

"If you feel that's the case, cousin, call the cops. You can use my phone."

Her lips narrowed into a thin line. "You know it is not our way to involve the *Englisch* law."

"Yeah, I do know that. The Amish don't like outsiders. Suits me."

"Is that what you were counting on? You're a man without scruples. You are a blemish on our family's good name."

Her biting comment surprised Paul. She might look small but she was clearly a woman to be reckoned with. She reminded him of an angry mama cat all fluffed up and spitting mad. He rubbed a hand across his mouth to hide a grin. His movement caught her attention, and she pinned her deep blue gaze on him. "Who are you?"

He stopped smiling. "My name is Paul Bowman. I'm an auctioneer. Mr. Hobson has hired me to get this property ready for sale."

Her angry gaze snapped back to Ralph. "I would like to see the document Eli signed giving you the farm that he had promised to me and my children."

"That document is none of your business. My attorney has it." He turned and walked toward the car.

She stifled her anger. Paul saw the effort it took and felt sorry for her. She drew a deep breath. "Ralph, please, search your heart and find compassion for us. You know Sophie will need medical care her entire life. I will be hard-pressed to pay for that care without the income this farm will provide."

Ralph stopped but didn't look at her. "The church will take care of you. Isn't that what they promise? Eli and I mended our difference. You should be happy about that. The Amish are all about forgiveness."

"I wish I believed you." Clara turned to Paul. "You can't auction off this farm. It doesn't belong to him."

Paul held up both hands and took a step back. "This is clearly a family matter, and I don't think I should get involved. Do you have a place to stay? My aunt and uncle will be happy to welcome you to their home."

Her tense posture relaxed a little. "I'm grateful for the offer but we have to stay here. My daughter has Crigler-Najjar syndrome. It's a rare liver disease. She has a special blue-light bed she must sleep in at night. It is upstairs in the front bedroom."

Paul had heard of the blue-light children but he'd never seen one. Clara's daughter was a pretty child with white-blond curly hair and a golden hue to her skin. Her bright blue eyes regarded him solemnly. The boy shared the same blond hair and blue eyes. He glared at Ralph but didn't speak.

Ralph gave his cousin a falsely sweet smile. "I don't have the keys to the house with me but you're welcome to sleep on the porch."

Clara's scowl deepened. "My child can't be without the lights. She needs to be under them for ten hours a day or risk brain damage. I have a set we travel with but I left them with my mother to be shipped here later. You must let us stay."

Paul heard the desperation in her voice. He caught Ralph by the arm. "This isn't right. Let her in."

Ralph jerked away. "You heard her say I'm a liar and a thief and you think I should help her? I'm going to call the sheriff and report her for trespassing. A night in jail might change her tune. Get in the car. I'm leaving."

Paul cringed. He was about to lose a sale that would have paved the way for his future business. He glanced around and picked up a rock twice the size of his fist. "Do you have the key, Mr. Hobson? If not, I'm going to owe you for a new padlock and a smashed door. I'm not leaving here until she and her *kinder* are safe inside."

Ralph pulled out his cell phone. "Go ahead. The sheriff can arrest both of you."

Chapter Two

Clara's jaw dropped in shock. Ralph was just the kind of man to make good on his threat. Would the *Englisch* law put her in jail? What would become of her children? Sophie had to have her light bed. Would the sheriff allow her to use it?

She had no wish for the young auctioneer to suffer because he was standing up for her and her children. She met the young man's gaze, ready to give in and leave if she could take Sophie's bed but Paul didn't look the least bit concerned. He winked at her, a sly smile lifting the corner of his mouth. What should she make of that?

He leaned toward Ralph and pointed to the phone. "The sheriff's name is Nick Bradley. Be sure to tell Nick it's Paul Bowman you want arrested. Nick's daughter, Mary, is married to my cousin Joshua. Oh, and tell him Mary is planning a birthday party for Nicky two weeks from Saturday. The picnic will be at Bowmans Crossing at six o'clock. You know what? Never mind. I'll just wait here with Clara and tell Nick myself."

With an angry growl, Ralph put away his phone, pulled a set of keys from his pocket and threw them at Paul. He caught them easily. "You'd do well to remember you work for me now. Get her out of here as soon as you can."

"*Danki.* I'll finish looking the place over and let you know in a couple of days when I think I can schedule your auction. Off the top of my head, I estimate six weeks. Maybe less."

Ralph nodded once. "Make it less. I need to get rid of this place as soon as possible. Inventory it from top to bottom and get me a copy of the list. Don't make me regret this. I can easily find another auctioneer."

"I'll do my best for you but if you're in a rush to get rid of the place, why did you turn down Mr. Jones without even hearing his offer?"

"I didn't like the look of the fellow." Ralph pointed at Clara. "I don't want her removing things she claims are hers without checking with me first but I want her gone as soon as possible. If she's not out of here in a few days, I will call the sheriff."

Paul glanced at her and then nodded. "I understand."

Ralph opened the car door. "Are you coming?"

"I can find my own way home."

"I'm staying at the Swan's Head Motel in Berlin until the sale is over." Ralph pulled out a business card. "This is my number. Don't believe a word that woman says. She's crazy. She imagines all kinds of things." Ralph got in, slammed the car door and sped away.

"I guess I won't need this after all." Paul tossed aside the rock and walked up the porch steps.

Clara stood and pulled a crowbar from behind her. "I reckon I won't need this, either."

He threw back his head and laughed. Clara settled Sophie on her hip as a smile twitched at the corner of her lips. Her son, Toby, was chuckling. It was a wonderful sound. It had been a long time since they had anything to laugh about.

"I reckon your cousin Ralph didn't think to padlock the toolshed." Paul grinned at her as she handed him the crowbar.

"He did," Toby said, putting the cat down.

"Mamm boosted me up to the window and I climbed in to get it."

Toby was so pleased that he had been able to help her. Ever since her husband's death two years ago, Toby had been trying to be the man of the family. A big undertaking for a boy of only eight.

Paul's face grew serious as he gazed at Toby. "Your *mamm* is blessed to have a son who is both agile and brave."

This stranger's words of praise to her son raised him another notch in her estimation. Toby stood a little straighter. "It didn't take much bravery. The spiderwebs were pretty small."

Paul smiled. "Agile, brave and modest, too. Just as a *goot* Amish boy should be. Your *daed* will be pleased when he learns of this."

Toby's shoulders slumped. He looked down. "Daed is in heaven."

Paul laid a hand on the boy's shoulder. "My *daed* is in heaven, too. God must have needed two strong Amish fellows to help him up there. I'm happy Daed is serving our Lord even though I miss him. I never forget that he is watching over me just as your father is watching over you. We must always behave in a way that pleases them, and I'm mighty sure that you pleased your *daed* by helping your mother today."

"You helped Mamm, too. Cousin Ralph would have made us leave if you hadn't been here."

Paul looked at Clara over Toby's head. "I think it would take a tougher man than your cousin Ralph to move your mother if she didn't wish to go."

Clara felt a blush heat her cheeks. She couldn't remember the last time a man had complimented her.

"Do you suppose your *daed* and mine are friends in heaven?" Toby asked. "I think he might be lonely without us and without his friends to talk to."

Clara bit her lip as she struggled to hold back the tears. Toby had a tender heart. He worried about far too many things. Adam had been a good husband but an indifferent father, preferring to spend his free time with his unmarried friends rather than the children.

Paul crossed his arms over his chest and then cupped his chin as he considered Toby's question. "Did your *daed* enjoy a good game of horseshoes and did he like baseball?"

Toby's eyes widened in surprise. "He liked both those things."

Paul turned his hands palms-up. "Then I

reckon they must be friends 'cause my *daed* liked horseshoes and he loved baseball, too. Would you do me a favor and take a quick look at the barn. I need to know if Ralph put padlocks on it."

"Sure." Toby took off at a run.

"You were very kind to my son," Clara said softly.

"Losing his father is hard for a boy that age to comprehend." Paul watched Toby for a moment and then turned to Clara. "And for his mother, too."

"How old were you?"

"Six. I'll get the door open. I almost wish you had produced the crowbar in front of Ralph. I would have given a lot to see his face."

It seemed he didn't want to talk about a painful time from his childhood and she respected that.

After unlocking and removing the padlock, Paul pushed the door open and stood back as she carried Sophie inside. The cat darted in and bolted into the living room. Clara set her daughter on a chair by the kitchen table, then turned to get her suitcases but Paul was already inside with them in his hands. "Where would you like these?"

"The black one can go on the bed in the room at the top of the stairs. The gray one goes in the room at the end of the hall. That door leads upstairs." She nodded toward it as she untied her black traveling bonnet and took it off. He opened the door and she heard him going quickly up the steps.

A quick glance in the mirror by the front door showed her *kapp* was on straight but her hair had frizzed at her temples. She smoothed them as best she could.

Paul Bowman was a nice-looking young man. He smiled easily, defended her right to enter the house and spoke kindly to Toby. She appreciated all that but even after hearing her say Ralph's trust had to be a fake, Paul was still going to work for her cousin. She wasn't sure what to make of that. Would he ignore her claim and auction this farm in six weeks? She couldn't let that happen. A handsome face and a few kind words weren't enough to blind her to the fact that he was helping Ralph cheat her children out of their inheritance.

She settled Sophie in the living room with one of her favorite books. The cat curled up at her side. Sophie had missed her pet while visiting her grandmother but happily, the bishop's wife liked cats and had taken care of Patches while they were away. Sophie was pretending to read the story to the cat but she looked ready to nod off. A nap would be just the thing for her. None of them had managed to get any rest on the long bus ride here. Toby came in to report everything was locked up tight. She told him to stay with Sophie when she heard Paul coming downstairs.

She joined him in the kitchen. "I appreciate your help, Mr. Bowman but I need to know your intentions."

He grinned. "My intentions are to stay single for as long as possible. Sorry."

She wasn't amused. "I'm talking about your intentions with regards to this farm."

"I'm an auctioneer. My intention is to inventory the property and ready the place to be sold." He quickly covered his head with his arms as if expecting to be hit.

She clasped her fingers tightly together. "Even after hearing that Ralph's claim to this farm is false?"

He opened one eye to peek at her. "That did give me pause but Ralph seems certain that he owns this place." He put his arms down and leaned one hip against the kitchen counter. "Is it possible your uncle changed his mind?"

"I don't believe Eli would do that to me. I will not let you and Ralph sell this place. I don't know how I can stop you but I will."

"Don't get riled at me. As an auctioneer, I have a responsibility to preform my due diligence by making sure that everything I sell is legal and as represented."

She crossed her arms. "What does that mean?"

"It means I won't sell a horse as a five-year-old if he has ten-year-old teeth in his mouth. I'll thoroughly check Ralph's claim of ownership. It may take a few days. In the meantime…"

"In the meantime, what?"

"I need to begin an inventory of the property."

"Why?"

"Because I have given my word to Ralph Hobson that I will handle the details of the sale for him. It's part of my job, and I have a reputation to consider. I can't say I hold much respect for the man after his actions today. No one should treat a woman and her children with such callousness. Unfortunately, he is my client."

"I'm sorry you have been placed in an awkward situation."

"*Danki*. Have you thought about where you will go?"

She planted her hands on her hips. "I'm not going anywhere. I'm staying here. This farm belongs to me."

"If you prove to be the rightful trustee, what are your plans for this place? Will you farm it? Rent it? Sell all or part of it?"

"I will sell most of the land but I plan to keep a few acres and the house to live in." Her uncle's death wasn't unexpected—he had been in poor health—but it still came as a shock. Maybe if she could make Paul understand how much was at stake, he would stop Ralph from selling the farm. It was worth a try.

"Crigler-Najjar syndrome is a fatal disease. I won't bore you with the medical details but a liver transplant is my daughter's only hope of living beyond her teens. A few months ago, I learned that I am an excellent match to donate part of my liver to Sophie. It's called a living donor transplant but it is a very expensive surgery. With all the testing and follow-up care, it will easily reach five hundred thousand dollars."

His eyebrows shot up. "Half a million?"

"*Ja.* Staggering, isn't it?"

"Won't the Amish Hospital Aid pay for most of that?"

Amish Hospital Aid was a form of insurance that depended on contributions from a pool of members each month. She was a long-time member and paid a modest monthly amount since before Toby had been born. Not all Amish approved of the method, preferring to rely on the alms contributed by their church members in times of need.

"Amish Hospital Aid has helped pay for Sophie's hospitalizations in the past. I paid the first twenty percent of each bill and they paid the rest. However, a liver transplant is not an emergency hospitalization. They won't pay for disability-related costs like her doctor's visits or her special lights. I have already sold my house and my mother sold her home to help pay for Sophie's future medical care. All I have to live on is the rent from my husband's harness-making business back in Strasburg, Pennsylvania, and the charity of church members. Eli's offer to come and live with him was a Godsend."

She blinked back unshed tears. "When we learned I could be a donor for my daughter, Eli altered the trust to leave the farm to me. He knew he didn't have long to live. He had cancer of the blood. The doctors told him a year or less."

"Why didn't he sell the farm outright and give you the money?"

"He was planning to do that once his crops were harvested this fall. Making me the beneficiary of the trust was a safeguard in case he died before that happened. Sophie needs a transplant before she gets much older. Every year, her skin gets thicker and that makes the blue lights less effective at breaking down the toxic chemical in her blood. Even a simple cold can put her life in jeopardy or cause serious brain damage because the toxin builds up faster when she's ill."

Would he help her or was she wasting her breath? She couldn't tell. She was exhausted and couldn't think straight anymore.

Paul rubbed a hand over his chin. "Unless you want Ralph to come back here with the sheriff in a day or two, you'll need to give me some idea of how long it will take you to move out."

Her hopes sank. He didn't care. "I told you I'm not moving."

"I heard you but we need a way to stall Ralph. He sounded adamant about calling the sheriff on you. We don't want that to happen and certainly not before I have his story checked out. I will insist on seeing a copy of the trust he claims to have and make sure it's real. I have no idea how long that will take."

Relief made her smile as she reached out and grasped his arm. "Then you believe me."

Paul didn't reply. His gaze remained fixed on her face. When she smiled, it changed her appearance drastically. The lines of fatigue and worry around her eyes eased, and she looked years younger. She was a pretty woman but more than that—she had a presence about her that was arresting and made a man look closer. She probably wasn't much older than he was.

She let go of his arm and clasped both hands together as a faint blush stained her cheeks. He liked to flirt with women and make them smile but he knew Clara wasn't in the mood to enjoy a little banter. He looked away and took several steps to put some distance between them.

It was surprising that he found her so attractive. She wasn't the kind of woman he was normally interested in. He liked to go out with girls who knew how to have fun. A widow with two children didn't make the list. He cleared his throat. "I believe you feel certain that you own the land. However, feelings aren't proof."

Her smile vanished. "At least you are willing to investigate Ralph's claim. It's a start. I'm not lying about Eli's intentions. My uncle kept all his important papers in his desk. I'm sure the trust papers are there."

Paul turned to face her. "You have them here?"

"I do. This way."

Paul followed her down the hall to her uncle's study at the rear of the house. The moment she opened the door, she stopped. "Someone has been in here."

"Are you sure?"

She looked around. "Every piece of furniture in this room has been thoroughly dusted. Eli didn't like me to clean in here and he wasn't this neat."

"I imagine the women of his church came to clean the house before the funeral." It was a common custom among the Amish to prepare the home for the service.

Obviously feeling foolish, she avoided meeting his gaze. "Of course. I should have thought of that. You must think I'm crazy to suspect someone has tampered with my uncle's possessions because the room is clean. The women wouldn't have disturbed the papers in his desk."

She opened the drawers one by one and went through them. Not finding what she was looking for, she went through each drawer again more slowly. "The trust document isn't here."

The trust wasn't there because Ralph had it. Paul kept that thought to himself. Ralph had warned him not to believe her. He hated to think Ralph was telling the truth about Clara's unbalanced state of mind.

She pressed a hand to her forehead. "What do I do now?"

She looked lost and desperate, as if she had reached the end of her strength. Paul fought the desire to put his arms around her and console her. It was highly unlikely that she would welcome such a move but he was compelled to offer a sliver of hope even if it was false hope. "Could your uncle have moved it?"

"I don't know why he would."

"If he wasn't feeling well and you weren't here, he might have given it to the bishop, his attorney or a friend for safekeeping so that someone would know what his final wishes were."

"Perhaps." She didn't look convinced. "I'll speak with the bishop and his friend Dan to see if they know anything about it. I don't know who his attorney was."

"I hate to suggest this but Ralph may be telling the truth. Your uncle might have changed his mind."

She shook her head, making the ribbons of her *kapp* flutter. "I can't believe that. Eli wouldn't leave us with nothing. Besides Ralph and my mother, the children and I are Eli's only family. He loved my children."

"I'm sure he did." She was vulnerable and sad. Paul wanted to comfort her but he didn't know what else to say. He chose to retreat. "I need to look around the property if that's okay with you."

"It seems I have no right to stop you." Her eyes filled with tears and one slipped down her cheek. She brushed it away.

Not tears. He hated to see a woman cry. He wanted her to smile again. He stepped closer. "Don't give up. Things will work out. You'll see. Maybe Ralph will have a change of heart and share the proceeds of the farm sale with you."

Her weary expression changed to a look of fierce determination. She squared her shoulders and rose to her feet. "I'll be very old and gray before that happens. Go and do my cousin's evil bidding. Make an inventory. Find out how much this place is worth so I'll know how much the two of you are stealing from my babies."

"I'm not stealing anything." Her sudden change of mood took him by surprise. Angry mama cat was back and spitting mad.

"You are if you help him! Get out!"

He made a hasty retreat to the front door and out onto the porch. He turned back to her, hoping to make her see reason. "I have a job to do."

"Then do it without my blessing." She slammed the door shut in his face.

Clara leaned her back against the closed door and took several deep calming breaths. Her heart hammered in her chest. She could feel the blood pounding in her temples. Allowing herself to become so upset served no purpose.

"What's wrong, Mamm?" Toby asked from the living-room doorway.

"Nothing." She moved to peek out the kitchen window. Paul was standing on the porch looking stunned. She wished she knew what he was thinking. One minute, he seemed compassionate and caring, tempting her to trust him. In the next breath, he said he was going to sell the property for Ralph as if that was the way things had to be.

It wasn't. She would find a way to stop them.

Her actions today ran contrary to her Amish upbringing and she was ashamed of that, ashamed her children had witnessed her behaving like a shrew. She had made a serious accusation against Ralph that she couldn't substantiate. Not unless she found the papers she knew had to exist.

Ralph possessed few, if any, scruples. This wasn't the first time he'd tried to trick or cheat an Amish family member out of money. This time it wasn't just about money; it was about Sophie's life.

Eli had wanted Clara to sell the farm when he was gone and use the funds to help Sophie. He had been a dear, kind man and she missed him deeply. She folded her hands together and sent up a quick prayer that God would be merciful to her and her children and allow her to grant Eli his final wish.

She went to search her uncle's bedroom next. She found a suit of clothes and his straw hat hanging on pegs. His work boots were sitting beside the bed on a blue oval rag rug, where he always kept them. It was hard to imagine he would never put them on again and tromp mud across her fresh-scrubbed floors. Brushing away a tear, she searched the single chest of drawers without success.

There was nothing in her bedroom or the children's rooms. She searched the kitchen and finally the large ornate bible cabinet in the living room. It contained only the family's oversized three-hundred-year-old German bible and a few keepsakes. There was nowhere else to look unless she got a ladder and went up to the attic. She couldn't imagine her uncle putting important papers where they would be so hard to access.

"Mamm, I'm hungry. Can I have a cookie?" Sophie asked.

"I don't have any cookies but I think I can find a Popsicle for you and Toby." Eli always kept a large box of assorted flavors in the freezer for the children.

The freezer compartment of the kitchen's propane-powered refrigerator turned out to be completely filled with frozen meals in plastic containers, all neatly labeled. The members of the church had made sure that she and the children would be taken care of when they returned. Clara took a moment to give thanks for the wonderful caring people in her uncle's congregation.

She found the box of Popsicles and gave each child their favorite flavor, then put out a container of spaghetti and meatballs to thaw for supper.

A knock at the door sent Toby rushing to open it. "Hi, Paul. You don't have to knock. You can just come in. Want a Popsicle? Grape ones are the best."

Paul stood on the porch with his straw hat in his hand. "*Danki*, Toby, but not today. I wanted to let your mother know I was leaving. I checked the generator and it's got fuel."

Clara moved to stand behind Toby. "*Danki.*"

She had forgotten to do that. Because the Amish did not allow electricity in their homes, Eli had gotten permission from his bishop to use a generator to supply the electricity for the blue lights Sophie needed. Eli had taken charge of keeping it running but she would have to do that from now on. She battled with her conscience for a moment but knew she couldn't lie.

"The generator belonged to Eli. You should add it to the farm equipment inventory."

"I'll try to remember but I'm a forgetful fellow. It might not make the list. I'll be back tomorrow. Is there anything you and the children need before I go?"

She hated to ask him but Sophie's health was more important than her false pride. "Would you start the generator so I can make sure the lights come on?"

"Of course." He started to turn away.

"May I come with you?" Toby asked.

Paul looked over his shoulder. "Sure thing. I can always use an extra hand. Come on."

The two of them had the generator started in a few minutes. Upstairs, Clara was relieved to see the lights come on when she flipped the switch. Eight blue fluorescent-light tubes were suspended above Sophie's bed by a wooden canopy that could be raised and lowered with a chain. Mirrors on the headboard, footboard and one side of the bed reflected the light all around her. Sophie hated sleeping under the lights. Clara let her go to bed with her favorite blanket each night but once she was asleep, Clara had to take it away so the light touched as much of her skin as possible.

After she was sure the lights were all working, Clara went downstairs. Paul was standing outside the kitchen door again. "Does it function as it should?"

"The lights all came on. Thank you for making sure the generator would run."

"You're welcome." He looked down at Toby. "I'll see you tomorrow. I might need someone to help me list all the machinery on the place. That is, if your mother doesn't mind."

Toby turned pleading eyes in her direction. "You don't mind if I help Paul, do you?"

She didn't want Paul coming back but he would in spite of her wishes. Telling her son he couldn't help would only hurt Toby.

"You can as long as you finish your own chores first," she conceded.

"I will." The happiness in her son's eyes relieved some of her reservations. He had taken a liking to the auctioneer.

Paul patted the boy on the head and smiled at her. "See you tomorrow then."

The man had a smile that could melt a woman's heart. Unless she kept a close guard on it, and Clara always kept a close guard on hers. Her life was filled with complications she wasn't sure she could manage. Adding one more was out of the question. She closed the front door as he walked away and then began sorting through the pile of mail waiting for her.

Paul did have a nice smile. She remembered

the sound of his laughter when she produced the crowbar and how gentle he had been when he talked to Toby about losing his father.

And this absurd line of thinking only proved how tired she was when a man's simple act of kindness had her thinking he was someone special. After a good night's sleep, she was sure she wouldn't find Paul Bowman half as attractive the next time she saw him.

Chapter Three

Early the following morning while the children were still asleep, Clara walked down the road a quarter of a mile to the community phone shack shared by the Amish families who lived in her uncle's area.

The small building that housed the phone and message machine was only six feet by six feet. It was painted a soft blue color and had large windows on two sides to let in the light. A solar panel on the roof provided electricity for the message machine. Inside was a narrow counter across one wall, where writing utensils and paper sat along with a copy of the local phone book.

A red light was blinking on the machine. She listened to the three messages. None of them were for her so she didn't erase them. Sitting on the single chair in the room, she placed a call to her mother's phone shack. She hoped her mother would be there to answer the phone. They had agreed on this time the last time they talked.

Her mother picked up on the second ring. Clara's throat tightened. It was wonderful to hear her mother's voice. "We made it safely back to Eli's farm. It was a long bus ride."

"How are the children?"

"They are doing fine. There was a letter from the Clinic for Special Children waiting for me when I got here. They did some lab work at her last visit. Sophie's bilirubin levels are holding steady with ten hours of light but we might need to increase her to twelve hours soon."

"Then the surgery can't be put off much longer, can it? Have you decided what to do with my brother's farm? It's hard to believe he is gone but what a blessing he has left for us."

Clara hated to share this news but saw no way to avoid it. "Ralph is here. He says Eli left the farm to him and he plans to sell it."

"What? Eli wouldn't do such a thing. He and I agreed you should have it."

"We know that but I can't find the papers Eli signed. Ralph claims to have them."

"That boy broke his mother's heart with his sneaking ways. I pray for him all the time. What are you going to do?"

"I thought I would speak to Dan Kauffman and see if he knows anything about this."

"The Lord has placed a heavy burden on you, dear. I wish I was there to help."

"I wish you were here, too. I miss you. The children miss you."

"As I miss them. Give them my love."

After hanging up the phone, Clara blinked back fresh tears. She had needed to hear her mother's voice, but it made her miss her even more.

Her mother, a widow, had moved from her home in Pennsylvania to live with a dear friend in Maryland after selling her house to help Clara pay Sophie's mounting medical bills. The two older women were like peas in a pod and got along famously. They made and sold quilts to a local tourist shop and enjoyed living by the sea.

When Clara had her emotions under control, she phoned Dan Kauffman next but no one picked up and he didn't have an answering machine. She hung up and decided to visit him as soon as possible. She needed to know where her uncle's trust papers were. They might not prove that Ralph's document was a fake but it would prove that she wasn't lying.

Let down because she hadn't accomplished anything, Clara started back to the house. She had only gone a short distance when she heard the clop-clop of a horse coming up behind her. A farm wagon drew alongside and stopped. Paul held the reins. He tipped his straw hat. "Good morning, Clara. May I offer you a ride?"

"I enjoy taking my morning strolls alone." She looked straight ahead and kept walking. She had managed to avoid thinking about him until now. He didn't pass her. Instead, he held the horse to a pace that matched hers.

"I think we got off to a bad start yesterday," he said after a long moment.

She chose not to reply, hoping he would get the message that she didn't wish to converse with him. He didn't.

Stopping the wagon, he got out and took the horse's rein to lead it as he fell into step beside her. "I hope you will accept my apology if I offended you yesterday."

"Are you still planning to auction my uncle's property for Ralph?"

He didn't say anything for a long moment but finally nodded. "I am until I have proof that he doesn't own the place."

She turned to face him and saw he had a horse and buggy tied to the back of the wagon. "Then I have no reason to accept your apology, for clearly you will continue to offend me. It's a wonder you can sleep at night knowing you'll be putting two small children out of their home."

She wasn't as angry with him as she was with herself. A night's rest hadn't lessened his attractiveness. She couldn't shake the annoying feeling that she liked him.

"Your sharp tongue slings some pointed barbs. Do you practice or is it a skill you were born with?"

She stared at him with her mouth open. No one ever talked to her like that. She snapped her mouth shut. "Perhaps you should move out of range."

"Can't."

She glared at him. "Do you need directions? Let me help. Get in your wagon and tell your horse to trot on. Within a minute or two, you will be beyond the sound of my voice."

To her amazement, he burst out laughing. "I admire your sharp wit even if I am the target of your jabs."

"Clearly, I have to be more direct. Mr. Bowman, go away."

"It's Paul. You must call me Paul because I'll be spending a lot of time at your place for the next few weeks. I need to finish my inventory of all the possessions, take measurements of the house, barn and outbuildings, inspect the fencing and determine the condition of all the fields. It could take me as much as three to four weeks to sort through everything. After that, it will take me at least another week or so to organize the items into lots for sale and tag everything."

She gave him an icy stare. "If my sharp wit offends you…leave. I am a woman with a serious and distasteful mission. The future of my children, Sophie's very life depends on proving that my cousin Ralph is a liar."

"Now you are wrong about one thing."

"You don't believe he's a liar?"

"I was raised to believe the best of every man until proven wrong and then such a man needs forgiveness and prayers. You're wrong if you think your sharp wit offends me. It doesn't. It's rather refreshing. You remind me of a mother tabby cat, all claws and hiss with her tail straight up and her back arched ready to defend her kittens at all cost."

Clara had absolutely no idea how to answer him except to say, "I don't like being compared to a cat."

"Sorry. I'll make a note of that. Is tigress or lioness a better comparison? Maybe not. I can see you're about ready to claw my eyes out. Should I stop talking?"

"*Ja*, stop talking," she said dryly, trying to maintain her anger but it was slipping away. His roguish grin and the twinkle in his eyes made it hard to resist his teasing charm. The most annoying thing was that she suspected he was well practiced at charming women.

He leaned toward her. "I predict we are going to be friends. You know why?"

"I don't have a clue."

"Because everyone likes me. I'm not bragging, just stating the truth. I'm a likable fellow."

She rolled her eyes. "And one who is in love with the sound of his own voice, I gather."

"Absolutely. See how well you know me already?"

He launched into the singsong chant of an auctioneer selling an imaginary hand-painted antique china teapot to an eager crowd of imaginary bidders. By the time they reached her uncle's lane, the price was over two thousand dollars. She had to wonder how he managed to take a breath while he was calling.

"Sold, to the bishop's grandmother for two thousand two hundred dollars and two cents. Please pay the clerk at the end of the auction." He grinned at her and Clara found herself smiling back as they stopped beside the hitching rail in front of her uncle's house.

She quickly regained her common sense. This handsome, smooth-talking man wasn't going to distract her from what she had to do.

"Sadly, I don't have a valuable antique teapot so I won't need your services."

"Are you sure about that? Have you done an inventory?"

Paul saw the indecision flash across her face before she composed herself. "I have not. After I prove the property is mine, I do plan to sell the farm and equipment along with some of the contents of the house."

"I'm sure you'll want an accurate inventory in that case. Why have it done twice? There's no reason I can't give you a copy of the lists I'm making now."

"I will need one, won't I?"

"Absolutely. If you want to ensure that my assessment is correct and complete, then perhaps you would like to assist me while I go through your uncle's possessions."

"While I hate to agree with you, you may have a valid point."

"And if we work together, you can be sure I won't hide the documents you need if I should find them."

Her eyes narrowed. "What makes you think I haven't already found them?"

He leaned close. "If you had, you would be shouting for joy from the rooftop."

A hint of a smile curved her lips. "I guess I would, at that."

He grinned. "See? I'm getting to know you better all the time. Where do you suggest we start our inventory?"

"You're going to let me decide? Aren't you the expert?"

"I will give you my opinion if you want. We should start in the attic and work our way down in the house."

Paul suspected that Clara was someone used to taking charge in whatever situation arose. He was willing to give her enough leeway to make her feel comfortable. He hated that he would be party to selling her home out from under her if Ralph did own it. He wasn't quite sure why it was important but he truly wanted her to like him.

There was something about her that touched him in a way no other woman had. He was afraid to examine his feelings too closely.

"I have no idea what is in the attic. I've never been up there," she said.

"I'm going to guess we will find cobwebs, spiders and maybe a mouse or two."

"If you are trying to frighten me, it won't work. I'm not afraid of spiders or mice."

"*Wunderbar.* Spiders give me the heebie-jee-bies. I'll let you deal with any we find."

She tipped her head as she regarded him. "I thought all men were tough and brave when it came to squishing insects."

"Nope. I never said I was a tough guy. I'll let you go first."

She stared at him for a long minute. She had something other than cobwebs on her mind. He said, "You might as well ask me whatever it is."

"Before we tackle this project, may I borrow your buggy for a short trip today?"

"I see you noticed that I brought one along. I did plan to leave it for you to use. I noticed Eli had one in the barn but the front wheel has a broken spoke and I don't know if Ralph will okay the repair. Do you want to borrow my horse, too?"

Her smile was brief but genuine. "*Ja*, I would like to borrow the horse, too. I looked but I couldn't find a harness to fit Patches."

He cocked his head to the side. "Patches?"

"Sophie's cat."

He laughed. "That's a *goot* one. My horse's name is Frankly."

"Frankly, not Frank?"

"*Nee*, it's Frankly and he's a bit high-strung. I'm sure you can manage him if you know ahead of time that he likes to try and turn left at every intersection."

"Why?"

"Frankly, he has never bothered to tell me that."

She cocked her head to the side. "Are you ever serious?"

"Not unless I have to be. Are you going to leave the *kinder* with me?"

She shook her head. "*Nee*, I'll take them with me."

"*Goot, kinder* are scarier than spiders."

Clara went to collect the children, leaving Paul waiting outside. She might have thought he was kidding about looking after the children but he wasn't. Toby he could manage but the needs of a girl Sophie's age were far outside his level of comfort. Paul was still standing beside the buggy when she came out with the children.

"*Danki*, for the loan of the horse and buggy, Paul. We should be back in an hour or two. Why don't you start downstairs and save the attic until I return?"

He hung his head and tried to look downcast. "You think I'm not brave enough to go into the spider's den alone."

She chuckled. "That's right."

"Paul is plenty brave," Toby insisted.

"Not as brave as your mother," he replied, meaning what he said.

He opened the buggy door and handed her up. He held her fingers a moment longer than necessary because he liked the way they felt in his hand. His eyes met hers and he saw them darken with some emotion before she looked away and pulled her hand free.

Clara blamed her fast pulse on the importance of talking to Dan Kauffman. She wasn't willing to admit Paul had such an effect on her. He was nice-looking, with his sincere brown eyes and light brown hair. In a way, he reminded her of her husband, Adam, but she wasn't looking to marry again. She needed to put all her time and effort into seeing that Sophie stayed well and providing for both her children.

She picked up the reins. "Frankly, walk on." As the horse headed down the road, Clara resisted the urge to look back and see if Paul was watching her.

When she reached the highway, Frankly tried to turn left, forcing her mind back to the task at hand. Once she straightened out the horse, she headed down the highway at a steady clip. Frankly had a high-stepping gait that made the miles fly by. He was the kind of horse young men wanted to pull their courting buggies so they could impress the girls. Was there someone Paul hoped to impress? She quickly dismissed the thought as none of her business.

Four miles from her uncle's farm, Clara allowed the horse to make his preferred turn to the left and entered the driveway for Dan Kauffman's home. She had only been to the place twice when she was younger but not much had changed. His wife still cultivated an extensive rose garden, and there was a large shaded pool with water lilies where gold and white koi fish made their stately rounds waiting for a handout.

She secured Paul's horse and allowed the children to go look at the fish while she walked up the graveled path to the front door. If anyone knew why her uncle had changed his mind, or if he hadn't, it was Dan. Although he wasn't Amish, he had been her uncle's closest friend since their boyhood days.

She raised her hand and knocked on the brightly painted red door.

Paul decided he would spare Clara the task of climbing into the attic with him. He was glad he did the minute he opened the trap door leading to the space. It was as dusty and cobweb-filled as he had suspected it would be.

An hour later, he hauled the last box of odds and ends down the ladder and carried them into the kitchen. Eli King had stored very few things in his attic. There were some books and a set of dishes with three chipped plates. There was a shoebox full of newspaper clippings. As an appraiser, Paul knew they were worthless but he set them aside for Clara to look through.

The final box contained a dozen carved wooden toys. They were dark with age but all in good condition. These were the kind of small items that usually sold well at an auction. He would have to ask Clara if there was a story associated with them. *Englisch* auction-goers particularly enjoyed purchasing an item with a history.

Paul made a list of every toy and noted the condition in the margin beside the description. When he was finished, he wasn't sure if he should wait for Clara's return or if he could go ahead and inventory the kitchen without her. As he was making up his mind to wait, he wandered into the living room and noticed a tall, beautifully carved bible stand in the corner.

It was made of dark oak and deeply carved with vines and leaves in the elaborate German style popular hundreds of years before. The sides and front of the cabinet were panels carved with bible chapters and verses in three-inch-high letters. On the front was Genesis 1:1. Below that one, a panel bore the inscription Isaiah 26:3. On the left side three panels were inscribed with John 3:16, Matthew 5:44 and Philippians 4:13. On the right side was Proverbs 22:6, Daniel 6:22 and Romans 12:2. Paul drew his fingers along the carvings. The verses must have held a special meaning to the cabinetmaker or the person he made it for.

Paul lifted the lid and stared at the huge antique German bible inside. The book was at least six inches thick and bound with red calfskin. He opened the cover and saw the publication date of 1759 on the yellowed page. Clara's family must have brought this bible with them when they immigrated to America with the first Amish families. This wasn't going to be sold. This heirloom belonged to Clara to be passed down to her children and her children's children no matter what Ralph Hobson thought should be done with it.

Paul heard the arrival of a buggy and glanced out the kitchen window. Clara had returned and his heart gave an odd little skip at the sight of her.

He pulled back from the window. This wasn't normal. He had dated plenty of young women and none of them had triggered a jolt of happiness, or whatever this was, when he saw them.

He walked outside, intending to take care of his horse but Clara was already unhitching Frankly. Should he take over or allow Clara to finish? He wasn't used to watching a woman do his chores while he stood idly by. "Did he behave for you?"

"He tried several times to turn without permission but once he understood what I wanted, we didn't have any trouble." She unhooked the last strap and led him out from between the buggy shafts. "But you will have to get a new buggy whip."

"What? You whipped my horse?"

"I'm teasing, Paul. Does he look like I beat him?" Frankly was nibbling at her black traveling bonnet. He pulled it off and tossed his head with it between his teeth.

Paul snatched it from the horse and handed it to Clara before he took the lead rope from her. "He doesn't look whipped but he looks like he is developing more bad habits. Maybe I should cut his ration of apples. Is it okay if I turn him out in your corral?"

"I don't see why not. I walked him the last mile so he should be cooled down. Good fellow. Thanks for the lift." She patted the horse's neck as he walked past her.

Toby and Sophie both had to pat the horse, who put his nose down to them before Paul turned him loose.

"Children, I want you to go play in the backyard."

"But I want to tell Paul about the fish," Toby said.

"Me, too," Sophie said. "They were gold and white and this big." She held her arms wide.

"You can tell Paul about them another time." Clara gave them a stern look. They walked away without arguing.

Paul unbuckled the harness and lifted it from Frankly's back. The tall black gelding shivered all over, happy to be unburdened. After hanging the tack on the wooden fence, Paul opened the gate and let the horse loose. Frankly trotted to the center of the corral. He put his nose to the ground and turned around in a tight circle several times before he laid down and rolled onto his back. He wiggled like an overgrown puppy scratching in delight. Paul would have to groom him again before putting him in a stall for the evening.

When the horse finally got to his feet, he shook all over, sending a cloud of dust flying about him. Paul realized that Clara had followed him to the fence and stood watching the horse, too. "Was your trip successful?" he asked.

"The man I went to see wasn't home. I left a note asking him to come and see me."

"Have you tried calling him? Almost every *Englisch* fellow has a cell phone these days."

"I did call his home but no one answered. He doesn't have a message machine. I don't think he has a cell phone."

She sounded depressed. He wanted to lift her

spirits but he wasn't sure how. She believed the farm belonged to her but Paul didn't see how she could be right. The Amish, like many *Englisch*, took great care to make sure their property passed legally into the hands of their heirs.

She pushed back from the fence. "What did you find in the house?"

"Twenty-two spiders, six mice, a box of newspaper clippings, several bags of material scraps and a box of old carved wooden toys. I decided to tackle the attic and show you how brave I am."

"I'm rather glad you did. I wasn't looking forward to it. Were the toys horses, cows, sheep and a collie dog?" she asked with a sad smile.

"That's exactly what I found."

"I remember playing with them as a child..." Her voice trailed away as a car turned in the drive. It was Ralph.

He and another man got out of the car. Ralph looked over the property with a heavy frown in place. "I don't see that you have gotten much done, Mr. Bowman."

"I have finished the inventory of farm equipment and I've started in the house. I'll begin moving the machinery out of the buildings and into the open tomorrow."

"I see you're still hanging around, Clara. Maybe this will hasten your departure." He turned to the man with him. "This is my attorney, William Sutter."

A distinguished-looking man with silver hair wearing a fancy *Englisch* suit stepped forward. "Good afternoon, Mrs. Fisher. I have here the signed and notarized trust document with the amendment attached naming Mr. Hobson as your uncle's heir, also signed and notarized. I hope this lays to rest any question about the validity of Mr. Hobson's ownership of this property. I was present at the signing and I assure you that your uncle executed this change of his own free will."

He handed the papers to Paul. Paul glanced over the documents and handed them to Clara. "It looks legal to me but I'm no expert."

"Fortunately, I am," William Sutter said without smiling.

Clara studied the documents and handed them back to Mr. Sutter. "This is not my uncle's signature. This is a forgery."

Hobson threw his hands in the air. "Unbelievable."

Paul stepped closer to Clara and spoke in Pennsylvania *Deitsch* so the two men could not understand what he was saying. "Be reasonable, Clara. A notary must have proof of the person's identity before affixing their seal. Without a driver's license, your uncle would have needed two people who knew him to vouch for him in front of a notary."

"I don't care what you say, that is not my uncle's signature." She switched to English. "Who vouched for him? I want to speak to the notary. Where can I find him or her?"

"I was one of the people who vouched for Uncle Eli." Ralph shoved his hands in his front pockets. "The other doesn't matter. Now you've seen the amendment and now you know the place is mine."

"I will never accept that my uncle deeded this property to you." She turned pleading eyes to him. "Paul, can't you see that he is lying? Tell me that you believe me."

Chapter Four

Clara desperately wanted Paul to say he believed her. Someone had to believe her.

He didn't. She saw it in his eyes. Ralph and his attorney were too convincing.

She was right and that was what mattered. But how could she prove it? She prayed God would show her the way.

Paul folded his arms over his chest and turned to Ralph. "I noticed an antique cabinet that contained a very old bible in the living room. I won't sell a family bible at auction."

"I want everything sold," Ralph stated firmly.

"If you don't want to keep it, then it rightfully belongs to Clara and her children. I will not sell it."

"It's mine and I want it sold!"

Paul shook his head. "I won't do it."

The attorney held his hands wide. "Gentlemen, is it worth squabbling over?"

His resolve evident, Paul said nothing. Ralph gave in. "Fine. It's hers. It's in German anyway."

Paul was confusing her again. He didn't believe she owned the farm but here he was standing up to Ralph over her family bible. She honestly didn't know what to make of him but she was thankful he understood the importance of keeping the bible in her family.

Paul pulled a notebook and a pen from his pocket. "I need to know who you want to do the land survey for property boundaries."

Ralph glanced at his attorney. Mr. Sutter smiled. "The sale of farm property doesn't require a new survey. The historical boundaries of the farm are adequate."

Paul looked skeptical. "Are you sure? It's unusual."

"Let the new owner pay for a survey if he wants one," Ralph said. "I'm spending enough to get rid of this place as it is." He pointed at Clara. "When is she leaving?"

"Never," she said.

"As soon as she can locate a suitable home for herself and the children," Paul said quickly. "Her situation is unusual given her child's special needs. Having her live here a while longer won't make any difference to our sale date."

Ralph looked ready to argue but his attorney forestalled him. "He's right. There's no point making waves. We want this sale to go smoothly."

Ralph's scowl deepened. "All right. Have it your way."

The attorney bowed slightly to Clara. "If you will excuse us, we must get going. We have another meeting." The two men went back to the car and drove away.

Clara stared at Paul. "That's it? You are just going to stand there and let Ralph get away with this?"

"I don't have a choice. He is the legal owner."

"The document they showed you is a forgery and I'm going to prove it." Her shoulders slumped as she realized he was looking at her with pity in his eyes.

"I'm sorry, Clara."

"*Nee*, you aren't. You wouldn't get your commission if I prove he's lying."

"I'm sorry you believe I would let that cloud my judgment."

She wasn't sure what to believe about him. Was he working with her cousin to steal her inheritance or was he the innocent party he appeared to be? She had no way of knowing.

She stiffened her spine. "Where are the items from the attic?"

"I left the boxes in the kitchen and put some things in the rubbish bin."

"I want to go through it all." She didn't meet his gaze.

"Of course."

If he sounded defensive, she could live with that. Sophie's life might depend on her making the right decisions here. She liked Paul but she had no way of knowing if she could trust him.

Two days later, Paul took a seat at the table in his uncle's kitchen while his family gathered around. His uncle, his brother, Mark, and his cousins Samuel and Joshua were present. His aunt Anna finished filling everyone's cups with fresh hot coffee and then took a seat at the foot of the table. Paul looked at them and took a deep breath. "I need some help and I'm not sure where to turn."

"This is about the auction you are holding soon?" Mark asked.

Paul nodded. "Ralph Hobson asked me to sell the farm he inherited from Eli King. Onkel Isaac, did you know the man?"

"Can't say that I remember him."

"He was Millie King's husband," Anna offered.

Paul turned to her. "Did you know the family well?"

"Not well but Millie and I served on a few committees together. The Haiti relief quilt-auction drive was one we both served on for several years. I think Millie passed away about five years ago. She never had any children, poor soul."

"Did she talk about her nephew or niece?" Paul asked.

"Let me think. I believe she said she had one *Englisch* nephew and an Amish niece who married a fellow from Pennsylvania. That's all I recall. Why?"

"Hobson thought the house was empty but his cousin, a widow with two children, has been living there for some time. She was away when Eli died so Hobson didn't know it. They each claim to be the rightful heir."

Isaac added a lump of sugar into his coffee. "This sounds like something the *Englisch* law must settle. Is there a will?"

Paul shook his head. "A trust. That's the real problem. Hobson and his lawyer have what they claim is a legal document making Hobson the new owner but Clara says her uncle's signature on it is a forgery. The papers that prove she gets the place are missing."

"What do you know about Clara?" Mark asked.

"Not much. She belongs to Gerald Barkman's church now. Her little girl has a genetic illness. She has to sleep under blue lights at night."

Anna pressed both hands to her cheeks. "Oh, how sad. My cousin Sarah in Pennsylvania had two boys who passed away from the same thing years ago. Children with the disease all die before they are grown. Such a hard burden for a young mother to bear. I will pray for her and her child."

"Actually, her daughter can live for many years if she gets a liver transplant," Paul said.

"Really?" His aunt smiled. "Then praise God for the doctors who do such work."

"Clara was counting on the sale of her uncle's farm to pay for the surgery. Now you can see why I'm sorry I accepted this job. It doesn't seem right to put her and her *kinder* out of their home and take away her daughter's chance to be well."

"We must care for widows and orphans as the Lord has commanded us to do. Is her church helping her?" Isaac asked.

Paul stirred his coffee. "I don't know. I assume they are but none of them have been around when I've been there."

Isaac pulled on his beard as he often did when he was deep in thought. "That doesn't sound like Gerald or Velda Barkman. They are good and generous members of the faith. I'm sure they will help her."

Joshua leaned back in his chair. "I think this woman needs an *Englisch* attorney but if this man has the law on his side, she will have to leave."

Paul turned to him. "Do you know an attorney who might help an Amish widow with limited funds?"

"What you need is an estate planning lawyer," Samuel offered. He was the oldest of the Bowman brothers and a thoughtful man.

Paul's hopes rose. "Do you know one?"

Samuel shook his head. "I don't. Sorry."

"Anna and I have worked with one to set up our wills," Isaac said. "His name is Oscar James. He has an office in Berlin. He might help. I will ask and let you know."

Paul looked at all their faces. "I guess the real question I want to ask is should I resign from this contract?"

"Did you accept it in good faith?" Isaac asked.

"I did but that was before I knew the situation," Paul said.

Isaac leaned forward. "Do you believe the man has the legal right to sell the property?"

"After the papers I saw and after hearing from his lawyer, I think he does but something about Ralph Hobson is off. He keeps stressing that he's in a hurry to get rid of the property but he could sell the place tomorrow if he wanted. It's *goot* farmland. So why did he hire me to set up an auction that will take weeks of work? Clara is his cousin. You would think he would help her instead of throwing her off the property."

Mark folded his hands on the tabletop. "Is the widow a pretty woman?"

Paul felt everyone's eyes on him. The heat began rising in his cheeks. "I hardly noticed."

Joshua nudged Samuel. "A telling answer if I've ever heard one. Paul notices every woman from sixteen to sixty."

"This isn't a laughing matter," Paul said. "Besides, I've only known her a few days."

His aunt laid her hand on top of his. "You must ask yourself if you truly distrust Mr. Hobson or if your dislike stems from the way he is treating his cousin. He has known her far longer than you have."

"He warned me not to believe what she said because she is crazy. She is a determined desperate woman but not a crazy one."

"A man's word is his bond. You must honor the contract you made with Hobson unless you have irrefutable evidence that he is cheating this woman," Isaac said. "Every man is a child of God and innocent until proven otherwise, even those we dislike. We cannot judge him. We can and will aid this young mother in whatever way is necessary to make sure she and her children do not suffer because of this situation."

All the men around the table nodded. It wasn't something they said; it was the way they lived their lives.

Paul sighed with relief. He knew this was what his family would say. Together they would find a way to take care of Clara and her children.

"Paul is here and he has the biggest horses I have ever seen." Toby left his place at the window overlooking the lane and ran to the front door.

Clara was busy drying Sophie's hair with a towel. "I want to see," Sophie said, trying to wiggle off the kitchen chair.

"You may go see after I am done with your hair. Toby, do not run near the horses."

"I know. I wonder if Paul will let me drive them."

"Don't pester him," Clara cautioned. "He has work to do. He is not here to entertain a curious boy."

"I'll behave," he said, shutting the door behind him on his way out.

Sophie crossed her arms in annoyance. "Toby gets to do everything."

"He gets to do more because he is older. When you are older, you will do more things, too." Clara closed her eyes and prayed that God, in His infinite mercy, would allow Sophie to grow old.

"How come boys get to do things that are so much more fun?"

Clara laid aside the towel and began the task of combing Sophie's long thick curly hair. "What kind of things do you mean?"

"Toby used to milk the cow and you never let me do it. He can throw hay out of the loft with a pitchfork and I can't."

Clara chuckled. "Most boys would consider those things chores and not fun."

"Then boys are silly."

"Sometimes they are." Clara tied Sophie's hair back with a ribbon and patted her shoulder. "Go outside now and let the sun dry your hair. You can watch but I don't want you to get in Paul's way. Is that understood?"

"Yup." She hopped off the chair and headed for the door.

"And stay away from the horses," Clara cautioned but Sophie was already out the door.

Clara finished cleaning up then moved to the sink and looked out the kitchen window. Both her children were standing on the fence at the corral watching Paul unhitch his team from the wagon. The huge caramel-colored Belgians, with their blond manes and tails, stood quietly as he worked around them.

She found herself as eager as her children to see Paul again but she resisted the urge to go outside. Her mind was in a constant state of turmoil where he was concerned. Such giddy foolishness over the mere sight of a fellow was better suited to a teenage girl, not a widow of twenty-eight with two children.

For the past few days, she had tried to sort out her feelings about him with little success. He was a hard worker. It was easy to see that. He enjoyed the children and took special care when they were around. He made them laugh. That was certainly a point in his favor. Once, she caught him enjoying a game of hide-and-seek with them. He would make a good father one day but why wasn't he married already? She had married at nineteen and was a mother by twenty. She guessed Paul's age to be twenty-four or twenty-five. Most Amish were married by the time they were twenty-two or twenty-three. Was he interested in someone? If she knew more about him perhaps she could decide if she should trust him.

She noticed him watching the house and she

stepped away from the window. No point in letting him think that she was interested in him. She wasn't. She had better things to do than gawk at him while he worked.

Her steadfast resolve lasted less than an hour. Before she realized what she was doing, she was back at the window watching him work and entertain her children.

She was relieved when he left in the early afternoon without speaking to her but she was quickly regaled with stories about him from Toby and Sophie when they came in. Paul was nice and funny and he knew everything about the machinery Eli had collected. Whatever his flaws, he knew how to endear himself to children.

The following morning, she left her uncle's ancient propane-powered washing machine chugging away on the back porch and walked around the house to check on her children. They were both sitting on one of Paul's draft horses. Their short legs stuck out straight from the horse's broad back. Sophie giggled when the horse reached around to nibble at her bare toes.

Paul was using the second horse to pull a broken wagon out into the sunlight from her uncle's shed. He had a dozen various pieces of equipment lined up along the side of the barn.

She could see it was hard work. His shirt was already damp with sweat. He had his sleeves rolled up and he stopped to mop his brow with them.

She went back into the house and made a pitcher of fresh lemonade. Stacking a few plastic cups together, she carried her offering to the corral fence. Paul had the wagon positioned where he wanted it. He dropped the lines when he saw her and came toward her. "I hope some of that is for me."

"It is. I see you found a way to keep my children out from under foot."

He leaned against the board fence, took off his hat and wiped his forehead with his shirtsleeve. "At least they won't get stepped on up there and Gracie is as gentle as they come."

"Mamm, see how high I am?" Sophie called out.

"I see. That's very high. How are you going to get down? I don't think I can reach you."

Sophie bent over to look at the ground. "I'm going to stay up here forever."

"Me, too!" Toby shouted.

"Then I reckon my fresh lemonade will have to go to waste."

Sophie held out her hands. "Paul, get me down. I'm thirsty."

He walked over and turned his back to her. "Come on, Goldilocks, change mounts."

She clasped her arms around his neck and slid off. Carrying her piggyback, he brought her to the fence and allowed her to step off beside Clara. Sophie grinned. "I like riding Gracie."

"So do I," Toby said from the horse's back.

Sophie looked at her brother and then at Paul. "Can we leave Toby up there forever?"

"That is a tempting thought but I imagine he is as thirsty as I am." He went back and lifted the boy off the horse. Carrying Toby under one arm, Paul toted the laughing boy to the fence and set him down.

Smiling at their antics, Clara handed them each a plastic cup full of ice-cold lemonade through the fence. She held up a cup to Sophie, who was straddling the fence but the little girl hesitated. "Will it make me turn yellow, too?"

"It won't make you turn yellow," Clara assured her. "It's good for you. It has lots of vitamin C."

Toby looked up at his sister. "Do things look yellow to you because your eyes are yellow?"

Sophie frowned as she considered the question. "The lemonade looks yellow but you don't."

Clara looked closely at the whites of Sophie's eyes. Whenever she had an episode of high bilirubin, Clara noticed the change in her eyes first. They were slightly yellow. More so than yesterday. Was her skin getting too thick for the light therapy to work?

Paul seem to notice her worry. "Is she okay?"

"I think so. Sophie, does your tummy hurt?"

"Nope. Can I have some more lemonade?" She held out her cup.

Clara relaxed. "You may."

Toby pointed toward the lane. "Mamm, I see the mailman. May I go get the mail?"

"I want to come, too," Sophie added, climbing down from her perch after leaving her cup on top of the fence post.

"You can both go. Make sure to watch for cars. Toby, hold your sister's hand."

"I will." The two of them took off together.

Paul finished his drink and handed the glass to Clara. "Exactly what is wrong with Sophie? Or does it distress you to talk about it?"

"It doesn't. You already know she has a rare genetic disease called Crigler-Najjar syndrome. Blood cells in our bodies are replaced constantly by new ones when the old ones die. As the old cells break down, they release a substance called bilirubin. That isn't a problem for people like you and I because we have an enzyme in our livers that turns bilirubin into a form that can easily be removed. Sophie was born without the ability to make this enzyme in her liver. When her cells break down, the bilirubin remains in her body and that leads to jaundice. We see it as a yellow color in her skin and the whites of her eyes. What we can't see is the damage high levels of bilirubin do to her brain, nerves and muscles. It can cause permanent brain damage and even death in a short period of time."

"How did this happen to her? Do you know?"

"Like her blue eyes, she inherited the defective gene from me and from her father. We were both carriers but neither one of us had the disease. It takes two genes to make the liver defective. It's very rare but it is seen more often among Amish and Mennonite children in Pennsylvania."

"How is it that Toby doesn't have it?"

"The doctors told us we had a one-in-four chance of having another child with the disease. God decides…as with all things in this world."

"Why do the blue lights help her?"

"That is the mystery of God's mercy. Light, particularly blue light, causes a reaction in the bilirubin in her blood beneath her skin. It changes it into a harmless product her body can get rid of easily. She needs to be under those lights for a minimum of ten hours every day. As she gets older, her skin will get thicker and it will take more hours to keep her level normal, and it will be less and less effective until it won't do her any good at all. At that point, she will die. Any stress, like a bad cold or the flu, can cause the bilirubin to rise high enough to turn her brain yellow. If that happens, the damage is permanent."

"What do you look for when she gets worse?" Paul asked, glancing down the lane at the children walking back from the mailbox.

"I must sound like I am an expert. I'm not. I only repeat the things they tell me. I don't truly understand the science. When her bilirubin goes up, she gets a yellow cast to the whites of her eyes first. She gets sick to her stomach and very tired. Sometimes she complains of pain in her stomach. When she does, I know it's time to take her to the doctor right away. If I wait too long, she can have seizures."

"What do the doctors do for her?" He sounded genuinely interested.

"They use plasmapheresis to quickly lower the levels of bilirubin in her blood."

He frowned slightly. "What does that mean?"

"It means they connect her to a machine that removes some of her blood and separates it into blood cells and plasma—that's the fluid in between our blood cells where the bilirubin stays. Then they replaced her plasma with some from other people, added back her own blood cells and transfused it all back into her. It takes a long time because they can't remove a lot of blood all at once. It helps but the effect doesn't last for long."

"It must be frightening to live with such a sentence hanging over your child."

"God is good. He is our protector and our salvation. I will do whatever I can for my baby girl but I know she is always in His hands. I grieve for what she must endure. I wish I could take the burden from her and carry it myself but that is not possible. I accept that."

"Isn't a transplant a cure?"

Clara took a deep breath. "A liver transplant will cure the syndrome. She will never need the lights again if the transplant works but she will need to take medicine to prevent her body from rejecting the new liver for a lifetime. The medicine is expensive. There can be serious complications. We may simply be trading one illness for another but I have to believe it will help her."

"I admire your strength in the face of such sadness."

"I look for the bright spot in every day. I try to teach my children to do the same. God is with us. Today, the bright spot was seeing Sophie up on your horse and her smile when you gave her a piggyback ride. To you, it might have been be a little thing. To me, it will be a memory to treasure for a lifetime."

The children came back from the mailbox with a single letter. It bore the return address of Clara's mother.

Clara took it from Sophie. "Toby, why don't you and Sophie go feed Patches. I forgot this morning."

"Okay." The children went up to the house.

Clara opened the letter. It contained a note from her mother and another envelope.

Her head started to swim at the sight of a familiar scrawl on the enclosed envelope. She grasped the fence behind her.

"What's wrong?" Paul bounded over the boards to stand beside her.

She looked at his concerned face. "It's a letter from Eli."

Chapter Five

"A letter from your *onkel*? How is that possible?"

Clara heard Paul's voice coming as if from a long way away as she stared at the envelope in her hand. A cold chill ran down her spine, making her shiver.

"Are you okay?" he asked, his voice stronger now.

She shook her head to clear the cobwebs from her brain. "I'm okay. It's just something of a shock. It's postmarked two days before he died and addressed to me at my mother's house."

Clara quickly skimmed her mother's note. "Mamm was as startled as I am to get the letter. She didn't mention it when I spoke to her on the phone. It must have come later."

"See what your uncle has to say."

Clara's fingers trembled as she tore open the envelope. She read his brief letter. "He asks about Sophie and goes on to say he had several visits from *Englisch* fellows wanting to buy his land. I can't believe this. He says he came home and found a man going through his papers. The fellow asked Eli his plans for the place after he was dead. He told the man his plan was to watch his crops grow from heaven." She looked up at Paul. "Why would anyone be that interested in this farm?"

"I have no idea. Does he mention anyone by name?"

"Nee."

"Don't you think he would've said something if one of them had been Ralph?"

"I believe you're right about that. He goes on to say he was concerned enough that he placed his extra cash, the deed and his trust document with Daniel for safekeeping."

She sprang to her feet and held the letter up to Paul's face, tapping it with her finger. "Do you see this? He says he placed some of his important papers, including the trust document, with Daniel. Not with Ralph and not with Ralph's attorney. This is proof that I wasn't making it up. I have to see Dan Kauffman right away. I can prove Ralph is lying. Now do you believe me?"

"It doesn't matter what I believe. It's what you can prove that matters. He doesn't say in this letter that he was leaving the place to you."

"*Nee*, he does not." Her elation drained away.

"Why did he think it was important to give the trust document to someone else? It has no value if someone were to steal it."

Clara shrugged. "I don't know. Maybe he knew it would be needed soon if he thought he was dying."

"Shall I hitch up the buggy and drive you to the Kauffman place?"

"*Ja*, that would be fine."

Clara clutched the letter to her chest. For the first time in days, she had hope, real hope that she could prove the truth about her uncle's intentions even if he didn't mention them in the letter. She hurried up to the house to get her bonnet and her purse.

Toby and Sophie were both in the kitchen. "Come on, children, we are going to see Dan Kauffman."

"We just went there the other day," Toby reminded her.

Sophie patted her hands together. "Can I see the fish again? I like them. Can I feed them?"

"Dan wasn't home so we are going to try to see him again today. Why don't you take some bread for the fish? Let me put your hair up right quick. Is it dry?"

Sophie ran her fingers through her hair and nodded.

Clara put up the child's hair and secured her *kapp* with several white bobby pins. Sophie grabbed two slices of bread from the table and then Clara hustled both children outside.

Sophie stooped to gather up Patches on the front porch. Clara shook her head. "The cat isn't coming with us."

"But she wants to see the fish, too," Sophie said hopefully.

"*Nee*, she stays here."

"Okay." Sophie put her down and the cat headed for the barn.

Paul sat in the driver's seat of the buggy with the reins in his hand.

"You don't need to come with me." It surprised Clara just how much she wanted his company. The thought was quickly followed by a mental reminder that she shouldn't depend on him. He would be gone from her life soon enough.

"I'd like to see how this mystery ends. I'm not staying here while you do all the great detective work."

Could she trust him? She wanted to but was that wise?

Maybe not but she was going to anyway. "Very well. I'm not in the mood to argue with you."

"I figured you'd tell me to mind my own business."

"I almost did." He chuckled as he helped the children in and then moved over so Clara could sit beside him. He clicked his tongue to get the horse moving and before long they were on the highway. He set the horse to a fast pace and for that she was grateful.

"What prompted you to let me come along?"

She looked down at her hands clasped together in her lap. "I'm not sure. I want to believe that you are not a willing accomplice to Ralph's plan."

"I will not aid him to do something illegal. I hope you find your proof."

She cast him a sidelong glance. "Why are you helping him? You have to know he isn't being honest."

"I gave him my word. I can't go back on that because I have learned to dislike him. What good is a man if he only keeps his word when it is convenient?"

It was an honest man's answer. She felt a growing respect for Paul. He was in an uncomfortable position because of her.

"You stand to make a lot of money from the sale, don't you?"

"I charge the standard amount for the industry in this part of Ohio."

"What will you do with your windfall if Ralph succeeds?"

"Most of the money will go back into my business. However, if we find proof that Ralph is lying and his documents are a forgery, I will not handle the sale. My reputation as an honest auctioneer and my scruples don't have a price."

"I'm sorry that you may lose money over this." She hadn't considered that her right to the property might cause Paul harm.

"Don't be sorry. The health of your *kinder* far outweighs any risk I am taking."

Feeling better about her decision to trust him, Clara settled back and waited impatiently to reach their destination.

When they turned into the Kauffman farmstead, Clara's heart began beating so hard she could hardly draw a full breath. She scrambled down from the buggy without waiting for anyone else and rushed up to the door and pounded on it. No one answered.

"Maybe he is out doing chores," Paul suggested.

Sophie tugged on Paul's arm. "Want to come see the fish?"

"Okay. Try the barn, Clara. I'll keep an eye on the kids."

"Danki." She scanned the farmyard for activity and started toward the large red barn.

Paul allowed the children to lead him to the koi pond at the side of the house. It was an impressive structure, made of concrete, and at least fifteen feet wide and twenty feet long. Water lilies in the center spread their large leaves and blooms on the surface and gave the fish a place to hide if they felt threatened.

"See the one with the white spot on his head, I like him best." Sophie tossed a piece of bread toward him but a quicker solid gold one got it.

"Stay back from the edge, Sophie. It's deeper than I thought it would be." He heard chickens cackling at being disturbed. Glancing past the trees around the pond, he spotted a woman coming out of a henhouse.

"Toby, watch your sister."

"I want to feed the fish, too."

"Okay, take turns." Paul saw the woman spot him and change direction to come toward him. He walked out to meet her. Clara saw her, too, and joined him.

"Are you looking for the Kauffmans?" The *Englisch* woman was tall and stout with short gray hair. She held a feed bucket in her hand.

Clara nodded. "*Ja*, I'm Clara Fisher. I need to see Dan. It's important."

"You are the one who left the note. I'm sorry I haven't been able to stop by. I guess you haven't heard. Dan suffered a stroke a week ago. I'm Opal Kauffman. Dan is my father. He's in the hospital in Millersburg. I just came by to take care of the animals, water my mother's plants and check on the house."

"I'm so sorry," Clara said. Paul heard the disappointment in her voice. It had to be frustrating for her to encounter another roadblock.

Would Opal allow them to search the house for the document Clara needed? "When do you think he will be home?"

Sadness filled Opal's eyes. "To be honest, his doctors give him only a slim chance for recovery. We are all having a hard time accepting the inevitable. What did you want to see him about? Maybe I can help you."

Clara clutched the sides of her skirt. "Your father was great friends with my uncle, Eli King. In his last letter to me, Eli said he placed an important document with Dan for safekeeping. Do you know anything about it?"

Opal slowly shook her head. "I don't remember seeing anything with your uncle's name on it but I haven't gone through Dad's things yet.

I will ask my mother if she knows anything about it."

"Perhaps we could look for ourselves?" he suggested.

Opal's eyes narrowed. "I don't feel right about letting you search the house. I will see Mom later today and ask her what she knows about this."

Clara folded her hands in a pleading gesture. "Couldn't you call her? It's vital that I find these papers as soon as possible. If you could just look for me, I would be eternally grateful. I wouldn't impose on you at such a difficult time without good reason."

The woman set down the feed bucket and pulled out her cell phone. "Okay. I'll see if Mom answers her phone. Sometimes she keeps it off when Dad is sleeping." She turned and walked a few feet away with the phone to her ear. Clara couldn't hear what she was saying.

Finally, Opal put away her phone and came back to Clara. "Mom didn't know anything about Eli bringing over papers for Dad. She said to tell you how sorry she is about your uncle's passing. He was well-liked by my family. She gave me permission to let you go in the house. I'm to help you if I can. What are we looking for?"

"The document is a trust, like a last will and

testament but it leaves the control of the farm to the trustee named without having to go through probate court."

"Sounds like something that he would keep in his safe. I have the combination. Let's go check." Opal opened the door and stood aside as Clara and Paul went in.

The safe in Dan's office held only a few items—a pocket watch and several pieces of jewelry. The only documents were insurance policies and the deed to the Kauffman property. A search of Dan's desk proved fruitless, as well. If he had Eli's trust, it wasn't in an obvious place.

"I'm sorry," Opal said as she showed them to the front door. "Mother and I will ask Dad about it when he comes around." Her voice cracked slightly. Paul suspected Opal was worried that might never happen.

"We appreciate your help," Clara said as they stepped outside. "Let us know if we can do anything."

"Mamm! Come quick. Sophie fell in the fishpond and I can't reach her." Toby skidded to a stop in front of them. "Hurry."

Paul bolted past Clara and reached the koi pond first. He jumped in and grabbed Sophie as she was flailing to keep her head above water. "I got you. You're okay."

He lifted the soaking child in his arms. Sophie clung to his neck, coughing and gasping for air. The water was only waist-deep on him but it was over her head. He slogged to the edge and handed Sophie up to Clara. She sank to her knees and held her daughter close.

"Is she okay? Do I need to call 911?" Opal asked, her cell phone at the ready.

Clara pushed Sophie's wet hair out of her face. She had a slight bluish tinge to her lips and she continued coughing. "I don't think so."

Paul plucked Sophie's *kapp* from among the lilies and heaved himself out of the pond. Water cascaded down his pants and pooled in his boots. It was going to be a cool ride home. He looked around for Toby. The boy was sitting a few feet away with his face buried in his lap and his arms wrapped tightly around his knees. His little shoulders were shaking.

"I'll get some blankets and towels." Opal hurried away.

Paul walked over to Toby and sat down cross-legged beside him. "Want to tell me what happened?"

Toby shook his head but didn't look up.

"Toby pushed me," Sophie said between coughing fits.

"It was an accident!" Toby shouted, looking up. His cheeks were stained with tears.

"Of course it was." Paul put his arm around the boy's shoulders and the child burrowed against his side.

Opal came running out with several blankets and towels. She and Clara swaddled Sophie. Paul accepted a towel and spoke softly to Toby. "Why don't you tell me what happened."

"She wouldn't share. I wanted to feed the fish, too. I was only trying to take the bread out of her hand. I didn't mean to push her so hard. She stumbled and fell in. I tried but I couldn't reach her."

"You did the right thing by coming to get help," Paul assured him.

"Is Mamm mad at me?"

"*Nee*, she isn't. She's happy you are safe."

"Will Sophie have to go back to the hospital? Mamm is always worried that Sophie will get sick. I never get sick."

Paul heard the unspoken part of Toby's statement. The boy believed his mother cared more about Sophie than she did about him. "Your mother depends on you a lot, Toby. She needs you to be strong because Sophie can't be. Let's go tell Sophie you are sorry."

"Okay." The boy rose to his feet and walked over to kneel beside his sister. "I'm sorry, Sophie. I didn't mean for you to fall in the water."

"That's okay. I forgive you. You can still be

my friend." Her speech brought on another fit of coughing.

Clara looked up at Paul. "We should get her home and out of these wet things as soon as possible."

He helped Clara to her feet and soon they all climbed into the front seat of the buggy. Clara kept Sophie in her arms while Toby squeezed in between the two adults. Opal stood beside them. "Let me know how she is. I've told my mother a hundred times that pond is too deep not to have a fence around it. My parents aren't used to having small children around here."

"She'll be fine," Clara said. "Don't worry your mother with this. Let her concentrate on helping your father get well."

Paul put the horse in motion and kept the animal to a fast trot once they reached the highway.

Sophie continued to cough. Paul thought her breathing was starting to sound labored. He exchanged worried glances with Clara. "She sounds worse."

"I know. I can feel a rattle in her chest. She must have gotten some of the pond water in her lungs. Stop at the phone shack and call for an ambulance. It's just ahead."

Paul stopped and got out. He made the call and then returned to the buggy. "They are on their way. Toby is welcome to stay with me and my family if that is okay?"

"That will be one less worry, *danki*."

"She's going to be fine. It's going to be okay." He didn't know what else to say except to reassure her and Toby.

It wasn't much more than fifteen minutes until they heard the siren in the distance but it was the longest fifteen minutes of Paul's life. He didn't understand how Clara stayed so calm.

Once again, he was reminded of what a strong woman she was. As the ambulance approached, Paul stepped out into the road to flag them down. Ten minutes later, Sophie was strapped to the gurney with an oxygen mask on her face. Clara sat beside her holding her hand. One of the ambulance crew closed the rear doors. Paul knew the man from his work as a volunteer firefighter. "Have Clara call me at my uncle's shop when she can."

"Sure. I'll let Captain Swanson and the guys at the fire station know. You'll have a driver when you need one."

"Thanks. That will help."

The man nodded, returned to the front of the ambulance and the vehicle sped away with red lights flashing.

Toby looked at Paul. "What's going to happen now?"

Paul pulled the boy against his side. "That is up to God. He has some fine men and women waiting at the hospital to help Sophie."

Clara's fears were realized in the emergency room as the doctors and nurses tended to Sophie. After looking at her X-rays, the physician in charge called it aspiration pneumonia.

"Depending on how much inflammation develops, this could be very serious. It wasn't clean water, it was more like a germ broth. She will likely get worse before she gets better. She's on oxygen now but her breathing is still labored. We've got her on some strong antibiotics and breathing treatments that will help. I understand she has Crigler-Najjar syndrome. Type one."

Clara nodded. "She does."

"I'd like to speak to her pediatrician. The syndrome is rare. I have not personally treated a case. I'm hoping her doctor can tell me how and if her syndrome will affect her treatment. Is she on phototherapy at home?"

Clara wrote out the name of Sophie's doctor and his phone number. "She stays under the lights for ten hours at night but I received a letter from her doctor telling me to expect to increase it to twelve hours a day before long."

"Is she on a liver-transplant list?"

"We are planning a living donor transplant. I am a match for her."

"I understand they've been doing wonders with this new technique since there are so few cadaver donors available. I wish more people would consider donating their organs but I understand why not everybody wishes to do that."

She could hear Sophie crying for her in the other room. Her daughter was too young to understand much English. The family spoke *Deitsch*, a German dialect at home. Most Amish children didn't learn English until they went to school.

"How long do you think she will have to be here?" Clara squeezed her fingers together.

"That's difficult to say. Forty-eight hours of antibiotics should show us an improvement. I will want her to have a two-week course to make sure this doesn't come back on her but the last week of that won't need to be intravenous. She'll be able to take pills. If you'll excuse me, I am going to try to have a conference call with her physician and several of the doctors on the staff here."

"Can I go back in with her?"

"Absolutely." He smiled for the first time. "We are going to take good care of her."

Instead of going directly back in, Clara called the phone number the ambulance driver had given her. It was Paul's uncle's furniture-making business. A woman named Jessica Clay answered the phone and identified herself as the secretary. As soon as Clara gave her name, Jessica said, "Hold on. Paul is right here waiting to hear from you."

"Clara? How is she?" The breathless concern in his voice was almost her undoing.

She fought back the tears. "As we suspected, some of the pond water went into her lungs and has caused pneumonia. They are going to keep her in the hospital. She could be here for two weeks. Less if she improves with the antibiotics they are giving her but it is too soon to tell how well they will work. I'm worried about her bilirubin. Anytime she gets sick it gets worse. How is Toby?"

"He's fine. Don't worry about him. He's playing catch with my cousin Joshua's daughter, Hannah, at the moment."

Clara was suddenly so tired she had trouble standing up. "I have to get back to Sophie. I will call you again tomorrow."

"Is there anything I can do? I feel awful. I should have been watching her."

She heard the deep regret in his words and knew how badly he must feel. "You are not to blame any more than Toby is. We must accept *Gott*'s will and pray for the strength to endure. If you need to do something, let Bishop Barkman know what has happened. He'll need to contact the district treasurer for the Amish Hospital Aid and tell him to expect a bill from the hospital. I will be fine. Take care of my boy for me. He likes a story at night before bedtime."

"I think I can manage that. I know some really scary ones."

"Paul, don't you dare."

"I'm kidding."

"I hope so but I wouldn't put it past you." She smiled as she hung up. He had a way of making her smile when she needed it the most. She thanked the nurse at the desk for the use of the phone and went back to sit with Sophie while they waited to move her out of the ER to a room.

"What did she say?" Jessica asked.

Jessica was the only person in the office with Paul. He repeated the information Clara had shared. "I wish I could do something. I feel terrible. I'm selling her house out from under her and now her little girl is in the hospital because I wasn't paying attention."

"Coulda, woulda, shoulda isn't helping." Jessica closed down her computer. "Think about what the woman needs and do it."

"Like what?" Paul asked.

"Really? Are all men so clueless?"

Annoyed, Paul sought to defend himself. "I can't stop the sale of her home."

"So, what's the next step?"

What was the next step? "She will need a new place to live."

Jessica smiled. "Now you're thinking."

"I'll let her bishop know her situation so her church can help."

"Good. What are her immediate needs at the hospital?"

"Clara can't stay awake around the clock to take care of Sophie but I know she will try. She doesn't have any family here to help her. Samuel's wife, Rebecca, has experience in caring for the sick. I wonder if she could help?"

Jessica took him by the shoulders and turned him toward the door. "Wondering is not doing. Go ask Rebecca. You're right, she has experience and she is the perfect person to aid Clara. Do Anna and Isaac know what has happened?"

"Not yet. I've been waiting to hear from Clara but I'll let them know after I've spoken to Rebecca. *Danki*, Jessica."

"Tell them I'll be happy to drive anyone who needs a lift. Consider me on twenty-four-hour call until further notice."

"You are a blessing to this family."

She winked at him. "And don't I know it. Get going."

On the short walk to Samuel and Rebecca's house, Paul pondered what else he could do for Clara. Without the money from the sale of her uncle's farm, she would have to delay Sophie's liver transplant. The Amish communities across the country were well-known for their fund-raising to assist with the special needs of their members. Paul had been an auctioneer for several such charity events. His cousin Timothy Bowman was currently the cochairman of the annual county fire department's fund-raiser. Timothy would be the one he should ask about setting up something to help with Clara and Sophie's medical bills.

After crossing the parking lot, he passed the new bakery and noticed Charlotte Zook standing in front of it, staring at the building. Her brown-and-white basset hound, Clyde, sat beside her. Charlotte's pet raccoon scampered toward Paul. He sidestepped her as she made a grab for his pant leg.

"Naughty girl, Juliet. Come here at once." Charlotte held out her hand. The raccoon raced back to her and climbed onto her shoulder. Mark was married to Charlotte's niece, Helen.

They lived with Charlotte across the river. "I'm sure Helen and Mark have gone home by now."

"I know." She and the dog continued to stare at the building. Charlotte was known for her eccentric ways as well as her unusual pets.

"Is something wrong?"

Charlotte tipped her head one way and then to the other side. "Juliet has decided this is a nice place to visit but she doesn't want to live here. I am trying to decide if she is right. I think she is."

Charlotte turned to him. "What has you so worried, Paul?"

He had no idea how she knew but she was right. "A friend's little girl is in the hospital with pneumonia."

"How sad. Do I know them?"

"The mother's name is Clara Fisher."

Charlotte shook her head slowly. "I don't believe we've met."

"She isn't from our church and she has no family here. I'm on my way to ask Rebecca if she can sit with little Sophie so that Clara doesn't have such a heavy burden to bear alone."

"That's very thoughtful of you. How old is her daughter?"

"I think she is four. Clara's son is eight."

"Such delightful ages. What do you think, Clyde?" She stared at the dog, who barked once. "I agree." Charlotte smiled at Paul. "Please tell Rebecca that Helen and I will be happy to help, too."

"I will, and thank you." He left her still staring at the building and headed toward Samuel and Rebecca's house.

On the way, he stopped to watch Toby and Hannah playing catch in front of Joshua's home. Hannah was a few years older than Toby and enjoyed taking care of younger children. Toby caught sight of Paul and raced toward him. He skidded to a halt a few feet away. "How is Sophie?"

Hannah came to stand behind him.

Paul kneeled to be on the boy's level. "Sophie is going to have to stay in the hospital for a while. That means your *mamm* will be staying with her. I hope you don't mind bunking with me until she goes home."

"I guess not." He didn't sound excited at the prospect but Paul wasn't offended.

"I know it's hard not to feel sad but this wasn't your fault. It was an accident. Sophie doesn't blame you and your mother doesn't, either. Remember how I said your *daed* and mine are watching over us?"

"I remember."

"Then you remember that it pleases them when we are brave and do the right thing."

"What's the right thing for me to do?"

Paul swallowed the lump in his throat and laid a hand on the boy's shoulder. "Keep on being the kind and helpful young man your mother expects you to be. Pray for your sister and your mother. Can you do that?"

"I guess. I wish I could do more."

"That will be enough. I'll make sure you get to talk to your *mamm* on the phone and I'll even take you to the hospital to visit her and your sister."

"Is the hospital far?"

"It is but my friend Jessica has a car and she has offered to drive us."

"Really?" Toby looked up from contemplating his feet.

"Really," Paul assured him. "I need to speak to my cousin Samuel and his wife. Hannah, why don't you show Toby the new kittens in the barn."

She grinned. "Okay."

"Toby, I'll need you to help me later with Isaac's horses. They need grooming."

"Even Gracie?" Toby asked eagerly.

"Even Gracie. Wait for me at the barn. I won't be long."

The two took off and Paul heard Toby telling Hannah about Patches. He rose to his feet. Somehow the boy had wiggled into a place in Paul's heart that he didn't know was vacant. The Lord had given Clara great challenges but He had given her great blessings, too.

Paul had never given much thought to having children. That was someday way off in the future but if he ever had a son like Toby, he would be blessed, too.

Four hours after arriving at the hospital, Sophie was finally asleep in her bed in the pediatric ICU. There were several small banks of phototherapy lights over her and a blanket-type fiber-optic light pad underneath her. She had IVs going in one hand and an oxygen mask on her face that she kept knocking aside while she slept. Clara finally ended up pulling her chair close enough to hold her hand. The wonderful nurses did everything they could to make sure they were both comfortable.

Clara realized she must've dozed off when she heard Paul's voice close beside her calling her name. She sat up and blinked several times to clear her vision. The clock on the wall said it was nine thirty in the evening. "Paul, what are you doing here?"

"I brought some help for you." He gestured to a tall, blonde Amish woman standing beside him. "This is my cousin Samuel's wife, Rebecca. She has had nursing experience. She will spell you so that you can get some sleep and if Sophie wakes up, she will have someone here who understands her *Deitsch*."

"Have you had anything to eat?" Rebecca asked. She had kind eyes and a gentle smile.

Clara shook her head. "Not since breakfast."

"Then my first nursing order is for Paul to take you down to the cafeteria and get you something hot to eat. You need to keep up your strength. But I don't really need to tell you that, do I? You've been through this before. You must let me know if there is anything I need to do."

Clara hated to leave but Rebecca was right. "Make sure that she keeps her oxygen mask on. She has a tendency to knock it aside."

"I will do that. We have also brought a pager. It has fresh batteries in it. If I need you, I or the nurse can call the number from the phone in here."

Paul moved to the door. "The pager will buzz no matter where you are. It will even reach outside for several hundred yards."

"How do you come equipped with a pager?" Clara glanced between Paul and Rebecca in astonishment.

"The Bowman men are all volunteer firefighters and have pagers to notify them when they are called out to fight a fire. This is one of the extras they keep on hand. Paul thought of it. He's not usually so bright." Rebecca smiled at him with a twinkle in her eye, taking any sting out of her words.

"I'm actually smarter than I look," he said in a hurt tone.

The women shared a speaking glance. Clara rose from her chair and walked past him. "I reckon I'll have to take your word for that until I see some solid evidence."

Paul held the door open for her and glanced back at Rebecca. "I'll see that she eats something."

They stopped at the nurses' station to let the staff know Clara had a pager and then they took the elevator to the lower level of the building. The cafeteria was almost empty. Clara chose a salad and a bowl of hot vegetable stew. Paul carried two cups of coffee to an empty table and settled across from her.

"How is she doing?" he asked.

"Her bilirubin level is climbing but the doctor believes the lights can keep it under control. I'm not so sure."

"They are prepared for that other treatment you mentioned if the lights don't work?"

"They are. Thank you for bringing your cousin's wife with you. That was very thoughtful."

"I had to. She insisted. If you don't know anything else about Rebecca, know that she gets her way when she sets her mind to something."

"I don't know how I can thank you for everything."

"We'll work something out. I like peach pie but apple will do in a pinch if there is ice cream."

She smiled at his teasing tone. "Why is it hard to get a serious answer out of you?"

"Because I don't have a serious bone in my body."

"I find that hard to believe. How is Toby?"

"He's worried. He feels badly but I put him to work taking care of our horses and that helped. He needed to be busy. He fell asleep on his cot before I had a chance to tell him a scary story tonight. My aenti Anna is keeping watch in case he wakes up while I'm gone."

"I'm thankful for that."

"I promised he could call you tomorrow and that I would bring him along when I come to visit. That should make him feel better."

It would make her feel better, too.

He pointed at her bowl. "Eat before your stew gets cold."

She did, only realizing after her bowl was half-empty just how hungry she'd been. She gazed at Paul and tried to separate the emotions swirling through her. There was gratitude but there was something else. Something more. Having him with her was comforting. She liked him. Maybe more than she should. Twelve hours ago, she had been wondering if she could trust him. Now, she couldn't imagine going through this without his help.

"Paul, I want you to know how much—" Her words were cut off by the sudden vibration of the pager in her pocket. She pulled it out and read the message that scrolled across the small screen. Fear clutched her heart.

Come to Sophie's room right away.

Chapter Six

Clara rushed toward the elevators with all thoughts of food forgotten. Paul was close behind her. She managed to catch the elevator door as it was closing. It opened revealing two nurses inside with trays in their hands.

"What floor?" one of them asked.

Clara couldn't recall the number.

"Three," Paul said, holding the door until she was inside and then stepping in beside her. "Clara, what's wrong?"

"The message said come to the room right away. I shouldn't have left."

When the elevator opened again, they hurried out and down the hall. Rebecca was waiting just outside the ICU doors.

"What is it? What's happened?" Clara pressed a hand to her heart, trying to stem her panic.

"Sophie spiked a fever and that led to a seizure. They were able to stop the seizure with medicine but they are concerned about her rising bilirubin levels."

"They will need to start plasmapheresis. Does the doctor know that?"

"Is that the blood exchange?" Rebecca asked. "That's what they are getting ready now."

"Can I go in?" Clara had been kept out of the ICU before when Sophie was ill in the past but she needed to be with her baby girl.

"You can go in. I just wanted to prepare you for what was happening. The doctor is pretty busy right now."

"Danki." Clara drew a deep breath to compose herself, pushed the button on the wall and went inside when the doors swung open.

Feeling helpless and useless, Paul watched the doors close behind Clara. He turned to Rebecca. The grim look on her face wasn't reassuring. "Will Sophie be okay?"

"That is up to *Gott*. Only He knows the answer. We must pray for the strength to accept His will no matter what it is."

"That's what Clara said but it doesn't seem fair that Sophie has to go through this. She is such a sweet child."

"All children are gifts from Him and precious in His sight. We are not meant to understand His plan in our time on earth. You are very concerned about them, aren't you?"

"Of course I am."

"It's a little surprising. You've only known them a few days."

"It seems like I have known them for ages. I can't explain it."

"She's not your usual type, Paul."

He gave her a puzzled look. "What is that supposed to mean? What's my usual type?"

"Lighthearted. Very pretty. Intent on having a good time by sneaking off to see a movie or going to a barn party."

"So?"

"Clara is anything but lighthearted. She has her hands full with the two children she has. She doesn't need another boy. She needs a serious and steadfast man as a helpmate."

"Now see, that's where you have it wrong. You think Clara and I have some kind of relationship going."

"Don't you? You practically insisted that I come here tonight. You went out of your way to provide her with the pager. You are looking after her son since she can't. That sounds like the actions of someone who cares very seriously about Clara and her children. Are you thinking of courting her?"

"Rebecca, stop trying to make this into something it's not. I'm glad that you and Samuel are happily married but not everyone is meant to wed. I'm working at the farm where Clara lives and that's it. I happened to be with her when Sophie fell in the water. I know the kind of trouble Clara is having so I'm trying to be a friend."

"There isn't anything wrong with showing someone how much you care or admitting how you feel."

He gave a dismissive wave with one hand. "This is the thanks I get for being responsible for once in my life? My family is ready to plan a wedding for me. Well, don't set the date because I won't be there."

"No one is planning a wedding for you. Samuel and I simply noticed you seem to be settling down and becoming more serious lately and we thought maybe Clara is the reason. Mark says you talk about her all the time."

Paul sighed. "If I don't seem as carefree as usual it's because I have troubles of my own and Mark is speaking out of turn. If I talk a lot about Clara it's because, through no fault of my own, I'm selling the property she believes is hers. How would you feel in my shoes? I wish the place did belong to her." He walked a few paces away and then came back. "I'd rather not talk about this now. How soon do you think we can see Sophie?"

"You should ask at the nursing desk. They will know."

Paul left Rebecca and went down to the nurses' station. Two nurses rushed past him and entered Sophie's room. He walked to the main desk and spoke to a woman with clouds and rainbows on her pink scrubs. "How is Sophie Fisher doing?"

"Are you a family member?"

"I'm not."

"I'm afraid I can only give information to her family. I'll have her mother come speak to you. There is a waiting room outside the doors. It could be a while."

"Don't bother Clara. I'll check back later." There was nothing he could do for her or Sophie now anyway.

He returned to Rebecca in the waiting area. "They won't give me any information. I'm not a family member. Tell Clara I decided to go on home. Will you be okay?"

"I'm fine. I will get word to you if anything changes. Jessica has agreed to be our messenger."

"Tell Jessica I appreciate her help." He left the building and found his driver, one of his fellow firemen, still waiting outside.

Later that night, as Paul lay in bed watching Toby sleeping across the room instead of sleeping himself, he kept replaying Rebecca's comments in his mind. Were others seeing something in his friendship with Clara that he didn't see himself? How did Clara feel about him?

He knew she couldn't stand him at first because he was working for Ralph but that wasn't where things stood between them now. For his part, he wanted to help her and the kids. She deserved her uncle's farm. She didn't want it for selfish reasons. She was trying to save her daughter's life. His need to pay off his trailer, repay Mark and improve his business paled in comparison to her goal. He needed the money the commission would bring but he would lose a lot less sleep over defaulting on his loan than he would over selling the farm with Clara's big, blue eyes watching his every move.

Early the following morning, he and Toby went down to his uncle's office to call the hospital. The operator rang him through to Sophie's room.

"Hello?"

The sound of Clara's voice dispelled the gloomy mood he was in. "Clara, it's Paul. How are things?"

"Sophie is resting well and her fever is down.

The antibiotics are doing their job and the blood exchange lowered her bilirubin level." There was relief in her voice as well as an underlying weariness. Was she happy to hear from him?

He wished he could see her face. "That's the best news I could hear. How are you holding up?"

"Trying to sleep in this recliner is like trying to sleep on a bed of rocks. They won't put a cot in here for me. Some sort of hospital regulation in the ICUs. I'm more grateful than you can know for Rebecca's company. I was able to go out and get some rest on the sofa in the waiting room while she sat with Sophie."

It pleased him that his actions had eased her way even a little. "I'm glad. Is there anything else I can do? Anything?"

"Sophie is worried about the cat. Can you check on Patches?"

"Sure. Toby and I'll be working at the farm most of the day. Tell Sophie not to worry, and tell her I miss her and..." He almost said "I've missed you" but stopped himself just in time.

"And?" she prompted.

"And I want her to get well quick," he added lamely. "Toby wants to say hello."

He handed the boy the phone and shoved his hands in his pockets while Toby chatted happily about his new friend, Hannah, the kittens and standing on a stepladder to brush Gracie's back. After a few minutes, Toby held out the phone to Paul. "Mamm wants to talk to you again."

Paul took the phone. "Toby's grinning from ear to ear. It did him a world of good to talk to you."

"You have no idea how much good it did me to hear his voice. Paul, I don't know how to thank you."

"I told you, peach or apple pie."

"You always find a way to make me smile."

"Then I'm doing my job. With all that is going on, don't forget to take care of Clara."

"I will try. I have to go, Paul, the doctor just came in. Goodbye."

"Goodbye," he said but the line was already dead.

He walked back up to the house with Toby skipping beside him. "What are we going to do today, Paul?"

"We're going back to your great uncle's farm."

"Are you still going to sell it?"

"I am."

Toby cast a sidelong glance at Paul. "I wish you wouldn't. It makes my *mamm* sad."

"Ah, Toby, I wish I wasn't the man Ralph hired for the job but I am. I must honor my commitment."

"Is it the right thing to do?"

Out of the mouths of babes. "I'm not sure, Toby. Sometimes it's hard to know what the right thing is. Why don't you fetch Frankly from his stall. I'll get him hitched to the buggy in a few minutes."

"I can harness him. I know how. Onkel Eli let me harness his horse."

Frankly was a docile fellow. He would be safe for the boy to work around. "Okay but be careful."

"I will." He took off at a run but before Paul could caution him again, he slowed to a walk.

Paul entered his uncle's house to find his aunt packing a basket with food. His cousin Timothy's wife, Lillian, was helping her. Anna glanced his way. "You look the worse for wear, Paul."

"I didn't sleep well."

"Worried about Clara Fisher?" Lillian asked in a lilting tone that suggested she already knew the answer.

"Is that so unusual?" He glared at the women in the room.

"Of course not," Anna said. "Lillian and I will relieve Rebecca and give Clara a chance to go home today if she wants. We are on our way to the hospital as soon as Jessica is free to drive us."

"Clara won't want to leave her daughter."

Paul thought of the panic in her eyes when the pager had gone off.

"We will be there to keep her company and to provide whatever help she needs. It will be a wonderful opportunity for us to become acquainted."

"I appreciate you doing this."

The outside door opened and his cousin Luke Bowman came in with his wife, Emma. Behind Emma came her youngest brother, Alvin Swartzentruber. Luke and his wife ran a hardware store not far from Bowmans Crossing.

"We heard about the little Fisher girl," Emma said. "What can we do to help?"

Paul looked at them in astonishment. "How did you hear about it?"

Emma moved past him into the kitchen. "Janice Willard, the midwife, ran into Rebecca at the hospital last evening. Janice stopped at our hardware store to get some lamp oil on her way home and shared what she knew. Anna, what do you need me to do?"

Anna looked over her supplies. "I've made sandwiches for Isaac and the men but if I am not home by supper time, they will need something. They're not very good at fending for themselves."

Luke chuckled. "They are much better than you think. As long as you believe they can't fend for themselves, they don't have to, and you will rush home to cook for them."

Anna looked taken aback. "In that case, I may stay away for a week."

Luke's smile vanished as he realized the implications of that statement. "Please don't."

All the women laughed at his discomfort. Emma walked over and patted his cheek. "Never fear. I won't tell them it was your idea if she makes good on her threat."

Luke looked relieved. "Paul, are you going over to work on your farm-sale property?"

Paul nodded. "I have to do it. I like the idea less and less but I'm stuck. The man owns the farm even if I wish he didn't."

Alvin stepped forward with a cell phone in his hand. "Luke says I should help you today. Anna, I'm going to write down my number for you. That way you can call me and give us information without our having to stop work to run down and check the message machine at the phone shack."

Anna patted his face. "I do not approve of young people having their own phones. You know that but since you are not yet baptized I cannot forbid you to use it. In this case, I'm actually grateful that you are willing to share this with Paul. Please put it away before Isaac sees it. He has stronger feelings on the subject.

Emma, could you run the gift shop while I'm gone today?"

"I can. Luke will manage alone at the hardware store."

"Paul, if you see Mark tell him I have the plate glass windows he wanted installed. We'll get them put in tomorrow."

Alvin kneeled and slipped the phone in his sock. He adjusted his pant leg and stood up. After writing down his number for the women, he followed Paul outside. Toby had Frankly tied to the corral fence and was nearly finished with the harness.

Paul walked around and inspected his work. "You did a fine job, Toby. *Danki.*"

Toby beamed with pride. Alvin finished harnessing the horse to the buggy and they were soon on their way.

An hour later, they turned into Eli's lane and stopped in front of the house. There was a car sitting beside the barn. It was empty. Paul scanned the area and saw a man in a white cowboy hat walking around the machinery that had been pulled out. It was Jeffrey Jones, the man who had offered to buy the farm from Ralph the day Paul met him.

Jones saw them. He flipped away his cigarette and walked toward them with an unhurried pace. "My dad used to use a corn planter just like the one out here. I knocked at the house but no one answered. Thought I'd look around a little while I waited."

"Waited for what?" Paul asked.

"Thought maybe I'd see if the owner has changed his mind about selling at auction. Will he be around soon?"

"I have no idea when he'll show up. He doesn't live here." Paul had an uneasy feeling about the man. He didn't look or act like a farmer so why was he so interested in buying this land? He turned to Toby. "Go open the corral gate for me."

The boy jumped out of the buggy and walked to the corral.

Jones pushed his hat up with one finger. "The young woman with the kids, she lives here, right?"

"She does."

"She is the old fellow's niece. I heard one of her kids is sick. I'm surprised the old man didn't leave her the farm. That would make more sense than giving it to a fellow who isn't Amish and who doesn't farm."

Paul didn't say anything. He nodded to Alvin. They both turned away and began unhitching the horse.

Jones chuckled. "I see you're going to give me the Amish silent treatment. I've had it before. I know when I've worn out my welcome. It's in my nature to ask questions. Sorry if I offended you." He tipped his hat and walked to his car.

After he drove away, Paul left Alvin and Toby to take care of the horse and crossed to the house. Like most Amish, Clara didn't lock her home. Paul stood in the kitchen doorway trying to remember how the room had looked the last time he was in it. A loaf of bread was still on the table. There were a few dishes in the sink. The room looked undisturbed. Patches was sunning herself on the back of the sofa.

Alvin peered over his shoulder. "What's wrong?"

"He was in the house."

"How do you know?"

He gestured toward the cat. "Sophie put the cat outside yesterday. She wanted to take Patches with her but Clara said no. Now the cat is over there by the window. She must have slipped in when he opened the door."

"That's creepy. Who is that guy?"

"I wish I knew. Where is Toby?"

"I put him to counting wrenches and arranging them by size."

"Okay. Let's finish the inventory of tools in the shed and then call it a day."

"Are you going back to the hospital?"

"I thought I might."

"To see the child or the child's mother?"

Paul scowled at Alvin. "What's that supposed to mean?"

"Nothing." The boy gave him an innocent grin.

Paul was eager to see Clara. She hadn't been far from his mind since he met her and that was starting to scare him.

He avoided serious relationships and with good reason. He had a hard time being serious about anything. He enjoyed being free to date whomever he wanted and whenever he wanted. He used to think being tied down to one woman was like having an auction without a loudspeaker. It was possible but it didn't make much sense.

He had five sisters at home, all younger than he was. He and Mark had grown up in a house full of women. The squabbles and petty arguments had been almost more than Paul could bear. Sure they all loved each other but they seldom got along. What did they argue about the most? Boys.

When Mark wanted to serve an apprenticeship with Isaac for two years, Paul had jumped at the chance to go along. Not only did it get him away from the foolishness of his sisters but it also gave him a chance to start earning enough money to begin his career as an auctioneer.

He liked women, he just didn't like the idea of being stuck with the same one for the rest of his life. What if she turned out to be boring or a nag? He had watched his sisters act coy and shy until the fellow they hoped to impress was out of sight. He always thought some poor fool was in for a rude awakening after he married one of them.

Paul vividly remembered some of the loud and scary arguments his parents had before his father's death. After retreating from the house following one of them, his father had laid a hand on Paul's head and said, "Don't be in a hurry to marry, son. There is no telling who your wife will become once you say 'I do.' Divorce is forbidden to us. One miscalculation and a fellow could end up regretting his choice for a long, long time."

Paul had a self-imposed limit of three dates with any given girl. More than that and they would start talking about weddings and babies. It would be a few more years before he was ready to have that conversation, if ever. So why was he in a rush to spend time with a woman who already had children?

The more he thought about it, the more he realized he'd spent too much time with Clara already. They hadn't been dating but they had seen each other almost every day for almost a week. He had no real reason to go to the hospital to visit her. He could send Toby with someone else. Clara had the women in his family to keep her company and support her. She didn't need him. That was a good thing. Wasn't it? So why didn't it feel right?

Paul turned and walked toward the toolshed. "You get started in here. I'm going to check the fences and the condition of the fields."

"Can I come with you?" Toby asked.

Paul shook his head. "Stay here and do what Alvin tells you."

A long walk alone was exactly what he needed to clear his head and gain some perspective.

He followed the perimeter of Eli's farm to make sure the fences were intact and in good repair. He found one place that needed to be mended and made a note of its location. It wasn't until he was on the far side of the property in the pasture on a rocky hillside that he came across something odd.

A new chain-link fence had been installed recently. Based on the fragments of the old fencing down the hill, the new fence was inside the farm's property line by nearly three hundred yards. Had Eli sold some of it to the mine? If that was the case, the land had to be surveyed even though Ralph didn't want it done.

Paul noticed a pile of rocky rubble near the fence. A closer look proved it was a drill site, and a recent one. Someone had been test drilling on Eli's land. The spot was on the far side of a steep ridge at the very end of Eli's property. The area was pasture and not farmed. It wasn't visible from the house.

"Can I help you, mister?"

Paul turned to see a man in a hard hat approaching from the mine buildings down below. He wore the uniform of a security guard for the New Ohio Mining Company.

"I'm not sure if you can help or not. I think this fence may be inside the property line of Eli King's farm."

"So what if it is?" The man stood with his arms akimbo, frowning at Paul.

"If it is, it will have to be taken down and moved back to the property line."

"Maybe you should speak to Mr. Calder. He's the boss."

"I'll be happy to. Shall I wait here?" Paul managed a pleasant smile.

"You'll need to call and make an appointment."

"Fine. Can you give me the number?"

"I'm not at liberty to give out personal information about the boss." The man turned and walked down the hill toward a cluster of buildings.

"I guess you're not at liberty to be friendly, either," Paul muttered.

He left the newly fenced area and followed Eli's old fence to the crest of the hill. A lone hickory tree marked the far corner. Paul caught the scent of cigarette smoke and stopped. There was no one about but there were several dozen cigarette butts littering the ground at the base of the tree. He picked one up.

Why would someone come out into the middle of nowhere to smoke? There was nothing here but a nice view of Eli's farmstead to the west and the mining company buildings to the east.

A feeling of unease made the hair at the back of Paul's neck prickle. Had someone been watching the farm? A gravel road ran along the other side of the fence. Paul assumed it wound around back through the hills to the mine but he wasn't sure. He'd never been on it.

Should he tell Clara about this? He didn't want to worry her. She had enough on her mind already. He didn't know for certain someone was watching the farm—they could as easily have been watching the mining company.

Most likely there was a simple and innocent reason someone had been waiting here. It wasn't unusual for a group of Amish teens on their *rumspringa* to meet at such an out-of-the-way place to smoke and enjoy music where their parents wouldn't see them. He decided not to mention it to Clara.

He finished walking the remaining fence lines and didn't find anything else out of order. When he reached the gate beside the barn, he saw a shiny black SUV turn into the drive and stop beside the house. A man in a gray suit got out and walked toward him.

"I'm Alan Calder. I understand you wish to see me. I own the coal mine you were snooping around today."

"I wasn't snooping and I didn't expect to see you so soon." Paul closed the gate behind him.

"I don't like to waste time. What can I do for you?"

"I think the fence you put up between your property and this one isn't on the property line."

"We didn't put up that fence."

"You didn't?"

"Eli King had the fence installed."

Taken aback, Paul wasn't sure he'd heard that correctly. "It would be unusual for an Amish farmer to install a chain-link fence across his pasture, not to mention expensive."

"I have no idea what is usual for an Amish

farmer. I understand this land is for sale. I'm willing to make a reasonable offer."

"It's going to be sold at a public auction. You are welcome to bid alongside anyone else who is interested."

"I doubt the new owner will get much for it. The place is a pile of rocks and weedy fields fit for goats and not much else."

Paul tipped his head slightly. That was the exact phrase Ralph had used when he first described the property. "Do you know the new owner, Ralph Hobson?"

Alan Calder frowned and crossed his arms over his chest. "Never met the man. Why?"

"Just wondering." Something wasn't right. There was no reason for the mine owner to rush over and speak to him. The man's demeanor seemed wrong. He looked ill at ease.

"Tell this Hobson fellow that I'm willing to make him a generous offer for the farm today as long as the sale includes the mineral right."

"I can give you his contact information."

"What is it?"

Calder immediately dialed the number Paul gave him and walked away speaking on his cell phone. The conversation quickly became heated by the sound of Calder's raised voice but Paul was unable to hear what was actually said. After a short time, the man returned to his car and sped away.

"Who was that?" Clara came out of the house and down the steps.

Had the sun come out from under the cloud? There wasn't any other explanation for why Paul's day suddenly seemed so much brighter. "What are you doing here?"

She grinned and tipped her head to the side. "Paul, I live here."

"I mean why aren't you at the hospital?" He tried to ignore the rush of happiness that filled his chest.

"Sophie is doing better and I needed to come home and get some things done. I've been wearing the same dress since we took Sophie to the hospital. It was starting to smell like old pond water. It was time for a change. Jessica drove me. She promised someone will be here at seven to take me back."

"That's great. How are you?" She looked fine to him. Better than fine. She looked wonderful.

He studied her lovely face. A light blush colored her cheeks, her eyes had dark circles under them but they sparkled now as she gazed at him. A soft smile curved her lips. She was happy to see him.

Rebecca's comment came back to him. Clara wasn't his type, so why was he so delighted to see her? He'd never felt this way around any other woman.

Suddenly uncomfortable, he hooked his thumbs under his suspenders. "I made a check of all the fences."

"Were there any problems?"

"What do you know about the mining company on the east side of this farm?"

"Not much. They wanted to buy or lease the mineral rights from Eli but he wasn't interested in selling. It seems they own the mineral rights under most of the land around here. People sold them ages ago. Dan Kauffman didn't know his grandfather had sold the rights in 1929 until underground blasting woke him up one night and he tried to get it stopped."

"Did Eli give someone permission to test drill out in the pasture?"

"Not that I know of. Why?"

"Because it looks like a test site has already been dug. That was the mine owner who just left. He wants to make Ralph an offer for the farm as long as it contains the mineral rights."

"One more thing he is taking from my children."

One more thing I'm helping Ralph Hobson take from them.

Paul pressed his lips together tightly. He wanted to beg Clara's forgiveness and promise he'd break his contract with Hobson. It might make her look more kindly on him but it wouldn't solve her troubles and it would only add to his. He had his brother to think about, as well. Mark and Helen couldn't open their business until Paul repaid them. Even knowing all that, Paul was ready to seek out Hobson and end their bargain.

His feelings for Clara were getting out of hand. He needed to put some distance between them.

The door of the house opened and Toby came out. "Mamm, can I stay with Paul again tonight?"

"I reckon that's up to Paul."

He rocked back on his heels and pasted a big grin on his face. "Sure. I'm glad to hear Sophie is doing better. I'd love to stay and visit but I've got work to do." The words came out sounding more abrupt than he intended.

A look of disappointment flashed across her face but it was gone before he could be sure. Her smile slipped a little. "Don't let me keep you."

She turned around and went in the house ushering Toby in front of her.

The letdown was massive. Paul didn't want to hurt her feelings. He didn't want her to be disappointed in him. He wanted to see her smiling again. At him. He took a step toward the house and stopped.

No, it was best to leave it this way. If she was unhappy with him, so much the better. That way she wouldn't harbor unrealistic romantic expectations.

Who was he kidding? Why would Clara harbor any romantic feelings about him? He was the joking auctioneer who was getting ready to sell the roof over her head. They barely knew each other. He should keep things professional and get things done as soon as possible. The less he saw of her, the less likely he was to open his mouth and say something stupid.

He found Alvin finishing up in the toolshed and said, "The barn is next. Let's go."

"I thought we were quitting early?" Alvin hurried to keep up with him.

"I have to get finished here before I make a fool of myself."

Chapter Seven

Paul was already hard at work in his uncle's shop when Mark came in the next morning. Paul continued sanding the top of a dresser while he waited for his brother to say something but all Mark did was raise one eyebrow and then get to work himself.

After about ten minutes, Paul couldn't take the silence any longer. "Aren't you going to ask me what I'm doing here so early?"

"It looks to me like you're working. That's what you get paid to do, right?"

"Right." He blew the sawdust off the piece he was working on and ran his fingers over it to test the smoothness. It would pass even his uncle's stringent quality requirements. "I'll go bring in some more particleboard and finish putting the backs on these dressers."

"Where is your little shadow?"

"Onkel Isaac took Toby and Hannah fishing this morning. I don't know which one of them was more excited."

"I'm going to say Isaac. When was the last time you knew him to take a day off?"

"Never. How is the bakery coming along?"

"Helen and I are moving into the upstairs tomorrow. We are still trying to convince Charlotte to come with us. She's decided Juliet doesn't want to move. I love the woman but she can be a trial. We are still waiting on the ovens before we set a date for the grand opening. Any idea when you can repay me? I hate to ask but I need to pay for the new picture windows that were installed and order baking supplies soon."

Sighing deeply, Paul faced his brother. "I'm sorry I'm holding you up. It was foolish of me to spend so much money on a fancy wagon that should have waited until I was actually making money at auctions. I let my wishful thinking override my common sense, if I ever had any common sense."

"Have you finished getting Eli King's farm ready to sell?"

Paul started sanding again. "I have a few things left to take care of."

"Such as?"

Paul threw down his sanding block. "Why is everyone so curious about Clara Fisher and me?"

Mark stopped work on the piece he was carving. "I didn't ask about Clara Fisher. What makes you so touchy on the subject?"

Running his hands through his hair, Paul struggled to find an answer. "I don't know. I can't get her out of my mind."

Mark crossed his arms and leaned against the corner of the unfinished desk behind him. "What makes you think you have to get her out of your mind?"

"I feel like I can't think straight. What's wrong with me?"

"Offhand, I would say you are smitten with the woman."

"I can't be."

Mark shook his head. "You're going to have to explain that one to me."

"She's not anything like the girls I go out with."

"Okay, right there is your difference."

Paul frowned at his brother. "What do you mean?"

"Clara Fisher isn't a girl. She's a woman. She's been married and widowed. She has children and one of them may die from a disease inherited from her mother. She might have been a girl at one time but she has been forged in the fire of life since then."

Paul thought of all Clara had been through and wondered how she could still face life with such a stalwart attitude. "Rebecca said Clara needs a strong and steady man as a helpmate, not another boy."

"Rebecca is probably right about that. She was widowed at a young age, too. She and Clara have a lot in common. Rebecca found love again and maybe Clara will, too. Paul, have you considered that you are looking at your feelings the wrong way?"

"How do you mean?"

"Instead of wondering if you are the right fellow or the wrong fellow or even if you should think about her as a potential mate, why don't you just be her friend."

"A friend?"

"Maybe she doesn't want a strong and steady helpmate to replace the man she loved. Maybe she just needs a friend to lean on until things improve. Stop trying to make sense of your emotions. Stop making this about you. Instead, concentrate on helping Clara through this rough time. If she is meant to find a new husband, the Lord will provide that man for her when the time is right. Until then, I think she could use your help without worrying if there are strings attached."

"But Rebecca said—"

Mark cut him off. "Rebecca is a wonderful person but she does have a tendency to meddle in other people's business. Don't let what she thinks influence you."

Paul considered his brother's words. "You're right. I don't have to make a decision about the rest of my life. I just have to help Clara when I can."

"That's right. I've known you to give a helping hand to a lot of folks. You're not as frivolous as you like people to believe."

"I appreciate you listening to me." Paul picked up the sanding block he had tossed aside and handed it to Mark, then headed for the door.

"Where are you going?" Mark called after him.

"To finish my work at the King farm before Sophie comes home. Clara doesn't need to see me counting each hammer and nail that should have been hers. Toby says it makes her sad, and that's the last thing I want to do."

Sophie improved slowly but steadily. Three days after her seizure, she was moved to a regular room on the pediatric floor. Clara was given a cot so that she could be with her daughter around the clock. It was a huge improvement over the uncomfortable recliner she'd been trying to sleep in.

On the morning of the fourth day, Clara woke to the sound of Sophie giggling. Clara lay still savoring the wonderful sound and giving thanks to God.

"Shh, we don't want to wake your *mamm*," a woman whispered.

Clara sat up and saw an older Amish woman standing next to Sophie's bed. The two of them had on hand puppets. Sophie's puppet was a raccoon. The woman held a long-eared dog puppet.

Sophie giggled again. "I'm quiet."

"It's too late—I'm awake." Clara sat up and stretched.

"It's about time," the woman said. "Juliet and Clyde are hungry for some breakfast. Clyde is so hungry he is going to eat Sophie's nose. Woof, woof, woof." The dog puppet scaled Sophie's arm, tweaked her nose then raced down her arm again.

The woman clapped her free hand to her cheek. "Oh, dear, what will you do without a nose, Sophie? You will never smell pancakes and bacon again."

Sophie tentatively touched her face. "My nose

isn't gone, Charlotte. It's right here. Mamm, see my puppets? Charlotte brought them for me to play with."

"I hope you have thanked Charlotte." Clara folded her blanket and tidied the cot.

"No thanks are necessary, dear. I am Charlotte Zook. My niece, Helen, is married to Paul's brother, Mark. He was Clyde's choice and a good one."

Charlotte held up the dog puppet. "This is Clyde. Of course, it's not the real Clyde but it does look something like him. However, my Clyde is much more beautiful and so very smart. This is the only dog puppet I could find with the long ears. Isn't that sad? I must write a letter to the manufacturer and insist they add a basset hound. I wanted to bring Clyde—the real Clyde, not the puppet—but I couldn't think of a way to get him into the hospital without being seen. They have the most ridiculous ideas about dogs not being clean enough to visit sick people. Why, they let people into animal hospitals all the time. Where is the sense in that?"

"I don't know." Clara had no idea where the conversation was going.

"Juliet would be much easier to smuggle in but I knew she didn't want to spend the day away from Clyde. They get very unhappy if they are apart. Clyde has been known to howl all night long when she is gone. Have you heard about the time Juliet went missing and then Mark married Helen and Juliet returned with her new family so Clyde didn't have to howl under Mark's window anymore?"

Clara stared at the odd little woman wondering if she was quite all right. "I have not heard the story."

"I must tell you all about it from the beginning."

"Not now, Aenti Charlotte," a young Amish woman said as she came in the door with a fast-food paper bag in one hand and a tray of coffees in the other. "I hope you like sausage biscuits, Clara. I'm Helen Bowman and you have met my aunt."

"Oh, I love sausage biscuits," Charlotte said. "Not as much as your croissants, of course. My niece is an excellent baker. She and Mark are starting their own bakery at Bowmans Crossing. I'm positive it will be a success. The smell alone will be wonderful in the mornings. I do miss those yummy aromas now that you and Mark have moved into your new home above the shop."

"I thought you were going to move in with us soon. We talked about it, remember?" Helen set the food and coffee on the bedside table.

"Juliet has made up her mind. She wants to

live near the woods on our side of the river. I rather like the blue lights Sophie uses, don't you? They are very pretty. I understand you have to move out of your home, Clara. I have a tidy place two miles from Bowmans Crossing on the far side of the river. You are welcome to move in with me as long as you like dogs and raccoons. I think we will get along wonderfully well, don't you?"

Clara wasn't sure what to make of the woman's offer. "I'll have to think about it."

Until now, Clara had refused to contemplate moving out of Eli's house but she was being stubborn and foolish. She had to have a plan.

"Does Clyde like cats?" Sophie asked. "I have a cat named Patches. I miss her a lot."

"Clyde loves cats and so does Juliet. How does Patches feel about raccoons?"

Sophie shrugged. "I don't know."

One of the nurse's aides came in carrying a tray. "Good morning, Sophie. I hope you're hungry this morning."

Clara translated. Sophie shook her head. *"Nee."*

The aide sighed heavily. "I guess I'll leave it here. Perhaps she will feel like eating later."

Clara crossed to stand by Sophie and pushed the bank of blue lights aside. "Is there anything that sounds good?"

"Dog food with a side order of raccoon food, please." Charlotte winked at the young woman and waved the puppet's paw.

The aide chuckled. "I'll speak to the kitchen right away."

"Sit down, Clara, and eat your breakfast. The *kaffi* smells *goot*," Charlotte said. "Helen and I are here to look after you today. Although I must say you look perfectly capable of looking after yourself. I'm not sure why Paul is so worried about you."

Clara began to straighten her daughter's bed. "Paul is worried about me? I think you mean he is worried about Sophie."

"*Nee*, he particularly said Clara Fisher has a heavy burden to bear and we must help her carry it. That's not at all like Paul. He has never asked me to help him carry anything before."

Helen cleared her throat. "Aenti, you should eat your breakfast."

"Not until after we feed Clyde and Juliet. They love eggs."

Charlotte handed a spoon to Sophie and then positioned the dog puppet in front of her face. "It's your turn to feed Clyde, Sophie."

Sophie put a small amount of egg on the spoon and held it toward the dog. Charlotte moved the puppet aside, ate the offered egg off the spoon and then whipped the puppet back in front of her face. "Yum. Yum. Yum. This is *wunderbar*," she said in a deep voice. The puppet rubbed his tummy.

"My turn." Charlotte picked up a fork.

Sophie giggled and held the raccoon in front of her face. Charlotte offered a bite of egg to the puppet. Sophie moved Juliet aside and ate the egg then made the puppet nod. "This is fine food for a raccoon," she declared in a high voice.

Clara, amazed at Charlotte's successful strategy, took a seat beside Helen on the cot. She ate her biscuit and sipped her coffee as Sophie and Charlotte continued the game until all the scrambled eggs and half the oatmeal was gone.

Clara looked at Helen. "Your aunt is quite remarkable."

"You have no idea. Wait until you meet the real Clyde and Juliet."

"Did Paul actually say he wanted to help carry my burdens?" She tried to sound indifferent.

"I'm not sure those were his exact words, were they, Charlotte?"

Charlotte used the puppet's paw to tap her temple. "Perhaps not his exact words but you know I often hear what people mean instead of what they say."

Helen nodded slowly. "I thought that might

be the case. Paul is concerned about you and about Sophie. He has had Toby helping him at the farm almost every day. The two of them are becoming inseparable."

A warm glow settled in Clara's chest. She tried to convince herself it was because she was thankful for the wonderful new friends she was making among Paul's family but she finally had to admit the truth. It was because Paul cared.

Clara leaned closer to Helen. "Was Charlotte serious when she offered to let us live with her?"

"This is the first I have heard of it but I think she is. Would you consider it?"

"Only as a last resort. I don't want to give up on Eli's farm."

The long days and nights at the hospital continued as Sophie gradually improved. Her biggest complaint was not getting to see Patches. She was convinced the cat was sad and crying for her. The time would have been unbearable without the cheerfulness of Anna, Charlotte's nonsense, Helen's kindness and the steady good sense of Rebecca and Lillian. Twice Anna brought Toby for a visit. He regaled her with stories of his time with the Bowman family. Paul let him help at the farm. Isaac took him fishing with his new friend Hannah, who could throw a ball as good as any boy. Paul let him harness Frankly and take care of Gracie.

Clara was happy Toby was enjoying himself but she wondered if her boy wasn't headed for a heartbreak. After Sophie was dismissed and the farm sale was over, Paul wouldn't have a reason to see the boy. Or to see her again. She didn't dare examine why the thought brought her to the verge of tears.

Clara enjoyed meeting everyone from the Bowman family but as the days wore on, the warm glow in her chest faded. She was left to wonder why Paul hadn't been back to visit.

Perhaps it was silly to want to see him but she couldn't help herself. She missed his cheerfulness and his teasing ways. It would be nice if she and Paul could resume their friendship once she was home again.

It was just friendship they shared. Clara refused to admit her feelings were stronger than that. She had known the man for less than two weeks. Any dependency that she felt was only because of the unusual circumstances they were both in.

It made a convincing argument, so why wasn't she convinced?

Perhaps Paul was seeing someone. Someone younger and without children. Without a complicated life. It was hard to imagine that an attractive and charming fellow like Paul didn't have a girlfriend. Who was she? What was she like? Was she pretty?

Clara shook her head at her own foolishness. It was none of her business if Paul had someone special in his life or not. The best thing she could do was stop thinking about him.

On Friday morning, eight days after Sophie's seizure, Clara received word that her child was being discharged. As much as she wanted to take her girl home, Clara was worried that Sophie's bilirubin level would rise. She could try to keep her child under the lights longer at home but she knew she would have a fight on her hands once Sophie started to feel better.

There was a knock at the door and a young woman in street clothes came in. She was dressed in a modern style, in a simple gray skirt and a white blouse with a touch of gray lace at her throat. Her blond hair was cut short and danced in springy curls around her face. "Good morning. I'm Debra Merrick, one of the public health nurses in this county. I was asked to stop in and visit with you about meeting Sophie's needs at home. I understand your daughter uses home phototherapy."

"She does."

Debra approached Sophie's bed and introduced herself in halting *Deitsch*. She looked over her shoulder at Clara. "That's almost the extent of my entire Amish vocabulary."

"That's not bad."

"I work with many Amish families in the Bowmans Crossing area. One thing I do fairly often is help Janice Willard, the local midwife, to get blue lights into homes for infants with jaundice. Amish homes without electricity present a unique challenge."

"I have a generator that runs through the night."

"That's good to know. I have not worked with a child Sophie's age. How does she do with her lights? Does she turn them off or get out of bed to avoid them?"

"Not often but I know she'll resent having to spend time under them at home when she feels like playing outside."

"Since I began working with Amish mothers, I have developed a particular interest in alternative treatments. There is some new research out on this topic. One study in particular caught my interest. It was done in Nigeria, where many people have little or no access to electricity. The study found that jaundiced babies who were placed in filtered sunlight did as well or better than babies under traditional blue lights."

"What do you mean by filtered sunlight?"

"A tent was constructed of a special clear plastic film that blocks the harmful rays of the sun and allows the blue light to come in. The babies didn't get overheated or sunburned."

"You think Sophie would benefit from this filtered light?"

"I do. As far as I know, studies haven't been done on children her age but I think it is worth a try. Is it something you would like me to look in to?"

"What does the doctor say?"

"Truthfully, he scowled and said he didn't know he was working in a third-world country. He hasn't been out of school very long. He'll learn that sometimes new ways aren't always better. The good thing is that sunlight doesn't require a doctor's prescription."

"How do we get this special film and how much will it cost?"

"I'm not sure. Do you want me to find out?"

"Would this replace her blue lights at night? What about in the winter?"

"It won't replace the blue lights but if it helps keep her levels lower longer, she might not have to spend as much time under the lights at night. We want to reduce the chance of brain damage until she can have a liver transplant."

"So we are only stalling for more time."

"That's one way to look at it. A transplant is still Sophie's only hope of a cure but we want to keep her brain healthy until that happens."

How long before Sophie suffered a bad cold or the flu or had another accident that would lead to her death? How long could she keep her beautiful baby girl before she had to return her to God?

Sophie's illness was God's will, and Clara accepted that. Determination was His gift to Clara. She used it to see that Sophie lived every day that He allowed. "Find out how we can make a special tent."

"Okay. I will be visiting Sophie at home once a week to see how things are going. I will also draw her blood for the lab studies if you agree to have a visiting nurse."

"I do and *danki*."

"When would be the best time for me to visit you next week?"

"Monday before noon, I think."

"That sounds great. It will take at least an hour to get her paperwork done before she is discharged so don't be in a rush."

"We've waited this long. We can wait a little more."

"Do you have a ride home?"

"I will need someone to drive us."

"The hospital has a list of people who volunteer to drive Amish patients. I'll have the nurse make arrangements."

After Debra left, Clara tried to keep Sophie entertained but she quickly grew bored. "Mamm, can I have a Popsicle? My throat hurts." It was her most frequent excuse for needing one. It was amazing how many sore throats had been cured by a single strawberry Popsicle.

"I will check in the kitchen to see if they have them. If not, will some orange sherbet make your throat feel better?"

"*Ja*, it will."

Clara walked down to the small kitchen on the pediatric floor and checked for Popsicles but didn't find any. She took a container of orange sherbet out of the freezer instead. When she walked out into the hallway she came face-to-face with the man she had decided not to think about again. "Paul."

"Hey. Hi." Being taken aback by Clara's sudden appearance before he was sure of what he wanted to say to her left Paul tongue-tied.

Clara seem to be suffering from the same malady. She looked down at her hands. "Hello."

Her voice broke the logjam in his brain.

Keep it light. Make it friendly. "Did I catch you sneaking to the kitchen for a snack?"

He was rewarded with a fleeting smile. "Sophie has become addicted to the orange sherbet."

"I can't say I blame her. I like the stuff myself. How is she?"

"She's getting crabby. I think it's time we went home."

"Samuel mentioned that Sophie might be released soon."

"And how did Samuel know this?"

"I would say the Amish telegraph but half the participants in the chain aren't Amish."

She tipped her head to the side "Explain."

He smiled, amazed at how happy he was to be with her again. How had he managed to stay away this long? "Your doctor told Debra, Debra told Janice, Janice told Rebecca, who told Samuel and Samuel told me."

"I'm surprised you didn't mention Clyde in there somewhere."

"I try to avoid that dog."

"I don't know the dog but his mistress is a very unusual woman."

"That's one way of putting it. Charlotte is unique."

"Sophie adores her. She invited us to move in with her. Was that your doing?"

"It was not. I thought she was going to sell her house and move in with Mark and Helen."

"Apparently, the raccoon doesn't want to move."

"She did mention that when I saw her last. Charlotte, not the raccoon. What do you think of the idea?"

"I will have to go somewhere if I can't find Eli's trust document but I haven't given up."

"I didn't imagine you would. Have you had any word from Opal Kauffman about Dan's condition?"

"He's here in the rehabilitation unit. I don't know more than that."

"Are you ready to go? I have a very excited boy waiting in the car with Jessica."

"Why did you leave him in the car?"

"Because of the surprise for Sophie. Can we go now?"

"You take this sherbet to Sophie and I'll check with the nurses."

Paul took the cup and peeked around the door into Sophie's room. She was sitting on the couch with puppets on both hands. A dog and a raccoon. If he had to guess, he would say that meant Charlotte had been in to visit.

For the first time, he noticed a yellow tint to the whites of her eyes. Would it go away or did it mean her condition was getting worse? The thought that she might die soon hit him like a felled tree. He blinked back tears, determined to present a cheerful face.

"Does someone in here want orange sherbet?"

Chapter Eight

"Paul!" Sophie's face lit up with a bright smile. "Come see my friends." She made the animals wag their paws at him.

He swallowed hard and walked over to her. "Clyde and Juliet are old friends of mine. Which one of them is going to eat this treat?"

She laid them aside. "Me."

He sat down on the sofa beside her. To his surprise, she climbed in his lap and cupped his cheek with her hand. "I've been missing you."

His heart swelled with emotion. "I've been missing you, too. Are you feeling better?"

She nodded. "I had a seezmure."

Paul looked up to see Clara watching them from the doorway. "She means a seizure," Clara explained as she sat on the arm of the sofa.

Sophie nodded solemnly. "I didn't like it."

He pulled her close in a tender hug. "I'm

sorry you had a seizure, little one. That must have been very scary."

"Mamm was crying and I got scared of all the people staring at me. I thought it would happen again. Will it happen again?"

"I don't know. I pray it won't."

"Want a bite of my sherbet?" She offered him a spoonful.

"You finish it. You're going home today. Toby is waiting downstairs."

"I'm going to ride in a car?" Her eyes widened with glee. "Can we go really fast?"

"As fast as the law allows," Clara said. "Eat up, the nurse will be here soon to take us down to the car."

When the nurse came in, Sophie happily hopped into the wheelchair for the ride down to the car. Clara and Paul walked behind her. Several nurses waved goodbye as she passed the main desk. Paul hung back while they got her wheelchair into the crowded elevator. "I'll catch the next one," he said as the doors closed.

A nurse walking past stopped. "Was that Sophie going home?"

He smiled. "It was."

The woman patted his arm. "Your daughter is a special little girl. We are all praying for her."

Rather than explain that he had no claim to

the child, he simply nodded and got on the next elevator that stopped.

Sophie and Clara were already out the front door when Paul arrived in the main lobby. He watched Toby get out of the car and run to hug his mother. "I missed you."

Paul had a moment to wish her smile for him had been as radiant as the smile she bestowed on her child. The thought was quickly followed by a hearty mental shake. There was no comparison between a mother's love for her children and her feelings for a friend.

Thrilled to have both children with her again, Clara hugged them until Toby complained that she was crushing him. When he and Sophie were settled in the back seat between Clara and Paul, Jessica turned around after lifting Patches out of a pet carrier on the front seat. "I think someone has been missing Sophie."

"Patches!" Sophie took the cat and cuddled her close. "I missed you so much."

Clara smiled at Jessica. "Thank you. She has been worried sick about her pet."

"Don't thank me. It was Paul's idea."

Clara turned to Paul. "It was a wonderful idea."

"Solid evidence that I'm smarter than I look," he said with a grin.

"I have to agree."

Clara caught sight of Opal Kauffman coming toward the hospital's front doors. She motioned to Paul and they both got out to greet the older woman.

"Opal, how is your father?" Clara asked.

Opal looked tired but happy. "He is doing amazingly well. His stubborn streak is finally paying off."

"I'm so glad to hear that."

"Do you think it would be possible for us to speak to him?" Paul asked.

Opal shook her head. "He isn't able to speak and he tires very easily. The rehabilitation staff are working with him, trying to teach him to write again. They are having some success. I have asked him several times about Eli but I'm afraid I couldn't get him to understand what I was asking. I'm hoping in time he will recover enough to communicate with you but I'm just so thankful that he has made it this far."

Clara hid her disappointment. "We must give thanks for every little blessing. Do let me know when he is able to answer my questions."

Opal smiled. "I will and I have convinced Mother to have a decorative fence put around the koi pond so what happened to Sophie can't happen to another child. Do you have a date for the farm sale yet?"

"If a date has been set, I haven't heard." Clara glanced at Paul.

"It will be four weeks from tomorrow."

Clara prayed that Dan recovered enough to tell her where the trust documents were before that fateful day arrived. What if she discovered them later? Did she have a right to the farm even after it had been sold? Maybe Paul knew the answer.

He decided to ride up front with Jessica so Clara wasn't able to ask him about it on the way home. As helpful as Jessica had been, she wasn't Amish and Clara was loath to discuss her personal business in front of an outsider.

When they reached Eli's home, Paul sent Jessica home and said he would find his own way when he was ready to leave. Clara quickly dismissed the surprising surge of joy his words brought as a combination of her own weariness and her happiness at having Sophie home. It didn't take long to get Sophie settled into bed for a nap with her lights on in spite of her resistance to being under them. Paul was able to coax her into taking a nap by promising a ride on Gracie when he came to work on Monday.

Back in the kitchen, Clara sighed as she sat down at the table. "It's good to be home. At least for a while. Would you like some coffee?" She started to rise again but he stopped her.

"You sit. That's an order. I'll make coffee."

"I can follow orders. I'm sitting. See me sitting?"

"I see you're about to fall asleep."

"I'm fine. Really."

"I'm going to scatter some pillows around your chair anyway."

She chuckled. "In case I pass out and fall out of my chair? That's not a bad idea."

Closing her eyes, she put her head back and listened to the sounds of Paul moving around her kitchen. It was a homey, comfortable sound. Like he somehow belonged in her home.

"Cream or sugar?"

"Just black, *danki*."

She rested until the aroma of fresh-brewed coffee grew stronger and she realized he was waving a cup of it under her nose. "I'm awake, I'm awake."

"Not so as anyone would notice."

She took the cup in her hands and savored her first sip. "Mmm, you make good coffee."

"Glad you like it."

"What do you have left to do here?" She wanted to know how much longer she could count on his company.

"Not much outside until right before the sale. Everything needs to be tagged and set up for people to view. I have an awning, tents and tables for that. I'll need to get auction announcements into the papers and farm journals as soon as I can. Four weeks isn't much notice for the general public. Most of what still needs cataloging is in here."

"And you can't do that while the kids and I are living in the house."

"Something like that. I'm sorry. This isn't something we have to talk about today. Get some rest. I'm going."

"Don't go." She didn't want him to leave. Tired as she was, she wanted to share these quiet moments with him but she didn't know how to explain it.

"Okay." He seemed to understand. He sat down across from her and sipped his coffee. For several long and soothing minutes, Clara relaxed and let the tension of the last weeks fade from her muscles.

When he rose to carry his empty cup to the sink, Clara decided to ask about the property. "What happens if the house and farm are sold and then I find the real trust papers?"

He shrugged, then folded his arms over his chest and leaned against the counter by the sink. "Honestly, I don't know but Isaac has an estate lawyer who should be able to answer that. I'll check with him."

"You've done so much for me already."

"That's not the way I see it." He stared at the floor for a short time and then looked up. "Is Sophie going to get over this illness, or has it caused damage that won't improve?"

"You mean to her brain?" Clara wanted to reassure him but she couldn't.

"I guess."

"I don't know. I assume she is going to get better until I see signs that show me she isn't."

"What signs?"

"Does she stay irritable? Does she have trouble remembering her numbers or how to button her coat? Those are the kinds of things I watch for."

"How do you do it? How do you live with this uncertainty and not fall apart?"

"I do fall apart. I try to do it behind closed doors with the windows shut, that's all."

"I'm serious."

"And I am being flippant. How is that for a role reversal? Do you use your teasing remarks and jokes to keep from answering serious questions?"

"You mean like you are doing now?"

She sighed. "I reckon I do. I don't fall apart because my children need me. I must be the one thing in their world that doesn't change. God is my rock and I am the rock of my family."

"I admire you tremendously."

"*Danki*, Paul. That means a lot to me."

"I'm glad. I'll be back on Monday. You know how to contact me if you need anything." She nodded, and he walked out the door.

On Sunday morning, Sophie felt well enough to go to church. Clara thought she was eager to tell the tale of her fall in the pool and her stay at the hospital to her friends. Clara drove the horse and buggy Paul had loaned her to Leonard Miller's farmhouse and arrived twenty minutes before the church service was due to start. Paul's thoughtfulness was one reason she had a hard time putting him out of her mind. Once the farm sale was over, it was doubtful she'd see him again. She would do well to remember that whenever she started looking forward to his arrival tomorrow. At least she knew she wasn't going to see him today. It was a relief knowing she didn't have to guard her emotions for a few hours.

As she turned her buggy over to the young men parking them and stabling the horses, she knew there would be plenty of questions to answer from those who hadn't seen her in weeks. She was greeted warmly by the women of the congregation in the kitchen when she carried in her basket of bread, jars of church spread and two fresh-baked apple pies. Although the congregation had not yet voted to accept her as a member, she had been treated with kindness by everyone from the first day she arrived.

Sophie clung to her side but Toby had already taken off to play with some of his friends outside.

"We hadn't heard that Sophie was out of the hospital." Velda, the bishop's wife, was slicing the pies at the counter. She put down her knife and came to kiss Clara on the cheek. "How is she and how are you?"

"We are both doing well."

Velda pressed her hands together. "God be praised. I know this is the news we were all hoping to hear. Paul Bowman notified us about the accident. Gerald has already contacted the Amish Hospital Aid treasurer. Are you able to pay the first twenty percent of the bill? If you can't, we will raise the money for you with a special alms collection."

"*Danki*, I will need help. I know I have the prayers of you and many more people to thank for Sophie's recovery. Perhaps Eli put in a good word for us, too."

"I am sorry for your loss," Velda said. "Eli was a dear friend to my husband. Many times Gerald sought Eli's counsel when he was troubled and he always came away feeling at peace.

Eli is with God now and we must draw comfort from that."

"I haven't asked but was anyone with him when he died?" She hated to think he had been alone in his final hours.

"Gerald and two of our sons went to check on him when he didn't come to the worship service that morning. They found him in bed. He was weak and couldn't stand. He didn't wish to go to the hospital so they stayed with him until he passed away quietly at about six o'clock in the evening."

"I'm so glad that he wasn't alone."

"I know you wished to be with him. He was grateful for all you did these past months. Was there anything missing when you arrived home?"

"Missing? Why do you ask?"

Velda's eyes filled with sadness. "The house was a mess when we returned from the burial. A few of us came back to straighten up before you got home. It looked as if someone had gone through the place looking for valuables. It is a sad testament to our times when a funeral published in the newspaper is an invitation for someone to ransack a house. I know it happens other places but this was the first time it has happened to someone in our church."

So Eli had been right to move his valuables.

"Do you know if Eli visited with the bishop while I was gone?"

"Gerald and our daughter took supper to him the Sunday before he died. They stayed and visited for a while. Why?"

Clara heard footsteps on the stairs and turned to see the bishop and two preachers coming down. The men normally met about thirty minutes before the service began and decided on the theme of their preaching for that day. None of them used notes. They preached as the spirit moved them, taking turns during the three-hour service. Their return from the meeting signaled the start of the preaching. Clara whispered, "I will tell you why it's important after church."

Like many Amish homes, the Miller house had walls on the lower level that could be moved back to make one large room for the preaching service. Amish prayer meetings were held in the homes of church members every other week. Backless wooden benches brought to the house in a special wagon were arranged in rows with the men sitting on one side of the room and the women sitting on the other. Some of the most elderly members were allowed to sit in cushioned chairs at the perimeter of the room. It wasn't unusual to see them nodding off. The youngest children sat with their mothers, who often had two or more under the age of three to keep quiet.

Clara took her place near the front among the married women with Sophie beside her. Toby was old enough to sit with the men. Before Eli's passing, Toby sat with him. Today, he and one of his friends sat near the back of the room with the unmarried boys. She hoped that he would behave but she wasn't above leaving her place to take him outside and admonish him if he was being inattentive. She had a moment of worry that Toby would find it difficult growing up without a man in his life but she gave over that worry to God and lifted her voice in song when the first hymn began.

Three and a half hours later, the final notes of the last hymn died away. The bishop addressed the congregation. "As many of you know, our little sister Sophie Fisher was in the hospital with pneumonia for more than a week. We give thanks to *Gott* that she is making a recovery. Her mother, our sister Clara Fisher, is a widow and dependent on us to help her with the burdensome cost of Sophie's hospital care. I ask that you give generously. Our deacons will now pass around baskets."

When the collection was finished, the congregation filed out of the house. The young boys and girls darted outside as fast as they could to start a game of volleyball. The men rearranged the backless benches into tables for the noon meal. The limited seating meant the congregation ate in shifts, starting with elders and ministers. The unmarried boys had to wait until the married men and married women had taken their turns. The unmarried girls were the last to eat.

Clara waited impatiently until the bishop finished eating. Before she could approach him, he began what turned out to be a lengthy conversation with one of the church members, who had a grievance against another member. When the bishop was finally free, Clara quickly moved to his side. "May I speak to you for a few minutes?"

He smiled at her. "Of course. It is good to see you. I'm told we raised several thousand dollars for you today. I will see that the hospital gets paid and what is left will be sent to you. How are you managing without Eli?"

"Well enough except for a problem brought about by my cousin Ralph Hobson."

"Ah, that one. Eli was always disappointed with his nephew. He felt that Ralph had great potential but that he chose a material path rather than a spiritual one."

Clara explained Ralph's claim to the farm

and her doubts about the validity. "Did Eli ever mention the farm trust he had created?"

"We talked about it years ago. I believe he wanted the farm to go to his sisters."

"That was the original arrangement but not long ago, he told me that he had changed the trust and left the farm to me so that I might care for my children. I take it he didn't discuss this with you?"

"*Nee,* he did not, although it sounds like something he would do. He was extremely fond of you and of little Sophie. He wanted to do everything within his power to help her."

"I believe Ralph's claim is a fake but I can't prove it unless I can locate the real trust."

"I wish I could help you. The only thing Eli mentioned recently that was unusual was that some strangers wanted to buy the farm. They were making a nuisance of themselves because they wouldn't take no for an answer."

"Do you know who they were? Do you have a name?"

"He was an *Englisch* fellow, that's all Eli said about him."

"*Danki*, Bishop Barkman." She tried not to let her disappointment show.

"Let us know if you need anything, Clara. You have only to ask."

Clara thanked the bishop and went to find

her children. At the barn, she told the boy looking after the horses that she was ready to go. He brought up Frankly and proceeded to hitch him to her buggy.

"Isn't that Paul Bowman's horse?"

Clara looked over to see Beverly Stutzman getting into her father's buggy. Clara had met the pretty young woman several times but they weren't really friends. "*Ja*, this is Frankly. Paul was kind enough to loan the horse and buggy to me until Eli's buggy can be fixed."

"I hope you don't mind a word to the wise. Paul Bowman is a fun, friendly fellow but he's not husband material."

"Since I'm not looking for a husband, perhaps that is a good thing," Clara replied with a stiff smile. She wasn't about to engage in gossip about Paul.

Her ride home was long and quiet. Sophie fell asleep for most of the way but woke with a start before they reached the house. "Mamm?"

"I'm here, sweetheart."

Sophie leaned against her side. "Where are we going to live when Mr. Hobson makes us leave our house? Will we live in a hollow tree?"

"A hollow tree? Where did you get that idea?"

"Charlotte said Juliet lived in a hollow tree."

"I'm not sure where we will go but it will be a lovely home because I will have my daughter and I will have my son and they will have their cat."

"Maybe we could live with Paul," Sophie said.

"That's a great idea, Sophie." Toby smiled from ear to ear. "Then maybe he could be our new *daed.*"

"We are not going to live with Paul, and I forbid you to mention such an idea to him. Do you understand me?" If her voice was too sharp, at least the children got the point.

"*Ja*, Mamm," Toby said softly.

Sophie nodded but didn't say anything. Her eyes glistened with unshed tears. Clara was sorry she hurt her child's feelings but she would die of embarrassment if Paul heard the children plotting to make him their new father.

"Paul said he was going to take me fishing," Toby said. "Can I still go with him?"

This was the first Clara had heard of the offer. Sophie scowled at her brother. "I'm not going to the fishpond anymore."

"We're not going to the fishpond. Those are tame fish. We're going to go fishing in the river. Paul has a boat and everything. We might catch a fish as big as a hog."

Sophie eyed him skeptically and then looked at Clara. "There aren't fish as big as an old hog, are there, Mamm?"

"There are, too, fish that big. Bigger. Fish in the ocean can be as big as our house. Hannah told me so."

"Who is Hannah?" Clara asked.

"My new friend. She's going to be in the sixth grade. Her *daed* is Paul's cousin. She has a baby *brudder* who is going to be one and they are having a party for him." He leaned toward Sophie. "Her grandpa is a sheriff with real handcuffs and everything. He could throw me in jail if I didn't mind Hannah. I was very good."

Clara smothered a chuckle. It was an unusual babysitting technique but it sounded like an effective one. "I'm sure glad you didn't end up in jail."

He sat back and nodded. "Me, too."

Paul will enjoy hearing this story. Clara sobered. Paul shouldn't have been the first person she thought to share the story with. It should've been her mother or even one of the Bowman women. The sad fact was, she spent far too much time thinking about Paul Bowman. How could she change it when she was going to see him almost daily?

The answer was painful, too. She would have to leave the farm and find somewhere else to live. She didn't want to do that but staying in the house was becoming pointless. It hadn't deterred Ralph's plans for the property. All she had accomplished was to fall for a handsome, smiling, smooth-talking fellow who liked her children and her cat. She wasn't normally a foolish person but she was turning into one where Paul Bowman was concerned.

That needed to change.

Chapter Nine

Paul harnessed his mare before daybreak on Monday morning and was soon on the road. Clara and the children were at home, and he was excited to see them again. He hummed a happy tune as his horse's rapid trot ate up the miles.

Clara was outside hanging her wash on the line. He pulled the horse to a stop in front of the house. "Did you finally get rid of the pond water smell?"

She laughed. "It took some scrubbing but I did. Go say hello to the children. *They* are looking forward to seeing you today."

An intense joy filled him at the sight of her smile. He longed to see her happy and the fact that he had made her smile filled him with a sense of accomplishment. "Where are they?"

"Putting a puzzle together in the kitchen."

He got out of his buggy and started for the front door but stopped when he heard the sound of car tires on the gravel lane. Ralph's car came into view. Paul's good mood faded.

Clara moved closer to him. "Just when I was beginning to enjoy the day. I know Ralph. He's going to start yelling about my still being here. That was his style even when he was a boy. Attack first."

Ralph brought his car to a stop beside Paul's buggy. There was no question that the man was angry as he stepped out of his vehicle. "I thought I told you to get her moved off my property. That was over a week ago. Why is she still here? If you can't get the job done, I will find someone who can."

Clara stepped forward. "You can't have known that Sophie spent the last week and a half in the hospital. She had pneumonia. She had a seizure. She was very ill. I didn't have time to look for somewhere new to live."

Some of Ralph's bluster faded away. "I'm sorry the girl was sick. That's not my fault. You can't keep staying here rent-free. And don't tell me you'll pay rent. I don't want a renter."

Paul tried to defuse the situation. "We have someone who has offered to let them live with her but there are no electric lines there and it would take some time to have them installed even if the bishop would give his permission."

"Use a generator. I thought that's what the Amish did."

"They are expensive to purchase," Clara said softly.

Ralph gestured toward the house. "You already have one."

Clara stared at the ground with her hands clasped in front of her. "Eli purchased that generator so it actually belongs to you, cousin."

Paul almost laughed at the honeyed meekness in her tone. Ralph threw his hands in the air. "Take the generator. I give it to you. Just get off this land. People will be coming to view the farm and I want them to be able to walk through the house without tripping over your kids or your cat."

"That's very generous of you." Clara inclined her head slightly. "It would be even more generous to return the farm to me."

Ralph ignored her and stepped up to Paul. "You have been dragging your feet, too. This place should be ready to auction today. Is it?"

"Advertising a sale this size takes time. The notices have gone to all our local papers. I have proofed the flyers and handbills with the printer in town. We are on schedule."

"Cut that schedule by two weeks."

Paul shook his head. "I can't. Not if you want it done right. The more people who hear about it and can plan to attend, the better."

"Plus it gives me more time to find my uncle's legitimate trust documents," Clara added, to Paul's chagrin.

Ralph's eyes narrowed. "I've made some inquiries about you, Bowman. You need this sale more than I do. Don't let your sympathy for my conniving little cousin sink your new business. Did you know that your loan can be purchased from your bank by someone else? I'm friends with a few people who have enough capital to do just that. Once that happens, any chance of getting an extension or refinancing goes out the window. I want you to think about that."

There was no mistaking the threat in Ralph's words. "I told you it would take six to eight weeks to be ready. I am pushing things to have it done in six weeks as it is."

"I'm not seeing the progress."

Paul took a deep breath so he wouldn't say something he'd regret. "I know you didn't want a new survey done but I think the coal-mining company that owns the land east of here is encroaching on your property."

"I don't need a new survey and I sure don't need you snooping into things that are none of your business. Don't make me sorry I hired an Amish auction service."

Paul regarded him steadily. "Given your obvious dislike of the Amish, I have to wonder why you did hire me."

Ralph took a step back and held his hands wide. "Did you think I picked the first auctioneer I ran across? I did my homework. You're young and your business is new. You've invested a good chunk of capital in getting it up and running. You stand to lose a lot if you can't get some money flowing in. I thought you'd be eager to do a great job for me as fast as possible. Don't jeopardize your future to impress my cousin."

Coming closer, Ralph smiled but it didn't reach his cold eyes. "There's an old Amish saying that goes something like this—'a man's good reputation is easy to lose and hard to recover.' What if I told folks things have been sold under the table or important items have come up missing? It would be your word against mine. Some of the Amish will believe you but not all your customers are going to be Amish, are they? Do you get my meaning?"

Paul understood but he didn't say anything.

"I see that you do." Ralph got in his car and drove off.

* * *

Clara moved closer to Paul as she watched her cousin drive away. She felt a chill in the air that hadn't been there before. "What did he mean?"

"He believes he has leverage he can hold over me to ensure I won't back out of our deal. If I try, he'll ruin my career."

"Can he?"

"A word here or word there about how I failed to carry off my first big auction, or how I took advantage of his lack of knowledge about farming to cheat him, and people will think twice about hiring me. All he needs to do is tell a few people I sold some of the best items before the auction even got started and my reputation will be in shreds. A man's reputation is everything in this business. In any business."

She laid a hand on his arm. "Are you in financial trouble?"

He lifted his straw hat and raked a hand through his hair. "Not yet but if I don't earn a hefty commission on this auction, I will be. I made some poor choices because I had too much confidence in myself and now I may have to pay for it."

She admired his honesty. "What are you going to do?"

He settled his hat low on his brow. "What can I do except hold the best possible auction and pray he lives up to his part of our bargain."

"I told you he wasn't trustworthy. You have seen how he conducts business. Do you still think the papers he holds are legitimate?"

He reached out to brush back a loose strand of her hair and tuck it behind her ear. The gesture was oddly tender and endearing. Her breath caught in her throat as she gazed into his eyes. A hint of a smile curved his lips. "You are brave to confront him. I admire your tenacity, Clara."

"I'm sorry I suspected you were helping my cousin rob me. Ralph has taken advantage of your honesty the way he has always taken advantage of Amish people in the past."

He grew somber as he stared at her. "Clara, I hope you know that you can count me as a friend."

"It's heartening to know I have a true friend at my side. I shall give thanks for that no matter how this turns out."

"It doesn't feel good knowing Ralph picked me to be his dupe but he is underestimating me because I'm Amish. It's true the Amish forgive those who have wronged us instead of reporting them to the authorities. I think he is counting on the fact that we won't report his actions to the law."

"You aren't suggesting we do that, are you? My bishop would not sanction such action."

"If you won't consider it, I understand, but you should know that Ralph Hobson isn't the only one with influential friends."

"Do you think your friends will help me?"

"I'm sure of it."

She closed her eyes and breathed a prayer that it might be true.

"Clara, my family is giving a birthday party for my cousin Joshua's son, Nicky, on Saturday. I thought perhaps you would enjoy spending the afternoon with us."

His abrupt change of subject puzzled her. "You are inviting me to a party? Like a date?"

Toby and Sophie came rushing out of the house. "Hi, Paul. When did you get here?" Toby was grinning from ear to ear.

Sophie took hold of Paul's hand. "You promised I could ride Gracie soon."

He picked up her daughter. "I don't have Gracie here today."

"Then can I have a piggyback ride?"

Paul lifted Sophie over his head and settled her on his shoulders. She squealed and knocked off his hat in the process.

"Just a little bit ago, I was asking your

mother to come to a birthday party. There will be games and other *kinder* to play with. I'm pretty sure there will be cake and ice cream. It should be a fun day. Do you think we can convince her to come?"

Toby looked at her with pleading eyes. "Please, can we?"

"It's very kind of you to offer, Paul, but I don't think we should. We aren't members of the family. It would be awkward."

"You already know my aunt, my sister-in-law and the wives of all my cousins. The men of the family are barely of any importance. Just ask their wives."

She smiled. "I think my time would be better spent looking for somewhere to live. I'm sure Ralph will have me evicted if I delay much longer."

"I thought you were considering moving in with Charlotte Zook?"

"She asked but I'm not sure she was serious."

"That's how most conversations with Charlotte go. If you are serious about looking for somewhere to live, then that is the perfect reason to come for a day. My aunt knows everyone. She'll help you find a place."

Clara nodded. "Okay, tell me how to get there, what time does the party start and what should I bring?"

"You don't need to bring anything."

"I am not showing up empty-handed."

"Then bring some treats that your own children enjoy and I'm sure the other children will, as well."

"Okay. We'll come."

The kids hopped up and down and clapped their hands. Paul favored Clara with a beaming smile. She felt a little bit like a kid herself. It was exciting to think about going to a party when her life had been bouncing from one crisis to another. It was exciting to think Paul would be there, too.

When Clara's buggy turned into his uncle's lane on Saturday, Paul was unprepared for the jolt of happiness that hit him. He ignored the warning bells that went off in the back of his mind. He was becoming much too involved with Clara. His idea of strictly being friends could become a problem if he couldn't keep his feelings for her under control. In spite of that fact, he walked out to greet her. "I see you found us."

"We didn't have any trouble following your directions," she said as she gathered her picnic basket.

Toby jumped down. "Where's the cake?"

Sophie gazed at Paul with her bright blue

eyes. "Where are Clyde and Juliet? I want to meet them. I have their puppets." She held the toys up for him to see.

"Clyde and Juliet aren't here yet but I know where there is some cake and ice cream just waiting to be enjoyed. Shall I tell you? It's a secret."

Sophie giggled and put both hands over her mouth. "I like secrets."

He leaned in the buggy and whispered, "So do I. Want me to tell you where the ice cream is?"

She nodded. He cupped a hand to her ear and whispered directions. He helped her out of the buggy and she took off at a run.

"No fair," Toby said. "I'm hungry, too."

"Better follow your sister."

Paul settled his hands on his hips as he watched Toby race to catch up with Sophie.

"You are good with *kinder*. My two are quite fond of you."

He grinned at her. "That's because I'm a kid at heart. Besides, I told you everyone likes me."

"Everyone except the string of Amish maids with broken hearts you've left behind you." Jessica Clay came up behind him. She was wearing a pink polka-dot dress. No one would mistake her for an Amish woman.

"You are simply jealous because I wouldn't go out with you, Jessica."

"Ha. I'm too smart to fall for the likes of you. I meant what I said about him, Clara. He never dates anyone more than three times."

Clara liked the outgoing *Englisch* woman. "I must thank you for your generosity in driving people and passing phone messages while Sophie was in the hospital. Don't worry that I will fall for Paul. I have already been warned that he isn't husband material."

"Warned? Who has slandered my good name?" His expression of pretend outrage was comical.

Clara arched one eyebrow. "Beverly Stutzman is a member of my church."

"Oh." His teasing manner vanished as a red flush crept up his neck.

"Busted," Jessica declared and walked away.

Paul helped Clara step down. "Beverly is a sweet woman but she's in a hurry to get married. I'm not."

Another buggy pulled up beside them. Charlotte sat in the front seat with a large brown-and-white basset hound beside her. A raccoon with a pink collar sat on top of the buggy making chittering sounds. Charlotte lifted the dog's front foot and waved it at Clara. "Clyde is delighted to meet you at last," she called out. "I have told him all about you and your daughter. We are looking forward to meeting your son."

The dog looked at Paul and woofed loudly. "Watch out for the dog," Paul said under his breath. "I meant to warn you about him."

"Is he vicious?" Concern for her children instantly took over Clara's mind.

"Not vicious but he does lack manners. He has a tendency to jump on people. I'm just warning you."

"He's certainly big enough to knock over Sophie or Toby."

"Don't ask me why but he likes to pick on adults. I'd never seen him misbehave around children."

That was a relief. Charlotte got out of her buggy and held her hands up to the raccoon. The animal jumped to her and quickly climbed to the top of her head. She lay down on Charlotte's *kapp* and began patting her owner's face with her little paws. Clyde lumbered ahead of them, occasionally stepping on his own ear in the process. He didn't seem to mind.

At the back of the large house, Clara saw lawn chairs had been set up in the shade of a hickory tree. The wide, well-kept lawn sloped down from a lush flower garden outside the back door of the house to the banks of the wide river. Downstream, she could see where a faded red–covered bridge gave access to the far bank.

Near the tree, a picnic table covered with a blue checkered cloth held a birthday cake with a single candle and several dozen gifts. She added her own offering for a one-year-old— six pairs of sturdy socks.

Anna waved and rose from her lawn chair amidst the group of women. A shout rose from the men in the horseshoe pit. Most of the men were either engaged in the game of horseshoes or watching and shouting encouragement to the participants. The exception was an *Englisch* fellow who lounged in a chair near the women. Clara noticed several of the partygoers weren't Amish.

Anna steered Clara toward an empty chair. "Let me introduce everyone you haven't met." She gestured toward an *Englisch* couple. "This is Nick Bradley and his wife, Miriam."

Clara was sure she had heard the name before but she couldn't recall where. Anna gestured to the young mother with a toddler on her lap. "You have met Mary but this is our birthday boy, little Nicky."

Mary smiled fondly at her child and then

looked at Clara. "Nick and Miriam are my parents and the reason my children are spoiled. My husband is the one who just made a ringer."

Clara glanced that way. "They all look like they are enjoying the game."

"The Bowman brothers manage to give every competition their all," Nick said.

It was fairly easy to pick out the brothers, for they looked alike with some variation in their hair color. She was finally able to match the husbands to the wives she had met except for one. Noah wasn't in the game but another man was. Clara hazarded a guess. "The tall, burly fellow is not a Bowman."

A woman with a baby about six months old in her arms laughed softly. "That one is my husband. You are right—he is not a Bowman."

"That is John Miller," Anna said. "He is a good friend as well as a good neighbor and a fine blacksmith. This is his wife, Willa, and his mother, Verna."

Willa shifted the sleeping baby in her arms so Clara could see him. "And this is Glen, who arrived last Christmas morning."

"A precious gift any day."

"You are so right," Willa said.

"And no party would be complete without the twins," Verna declared as a pair of girls raced up to her chair. "Lucy and Megan, this is Clara Fisher."

"Hello," they said in unison.

Clara smiled at them. "Are you enjoying the party?"

"Yup," one of them said.

The two blonde, blue-eyed girls were carbon copies of each other. Clara couldn't tell them apart. They kneeled on a blue-and-white patchwork quilt spread on the grass in front of the chairs. Sophie sat shyly to one side with her arm around Clyde. The dog seemed well-behaved to Clara.

"Toby said you have yellow eyes," one of the twins said and moved closer to Sophie.

The other twin leaned in, too. "They don't look yellow to me. They look blue."

"They only get yellow when I'm sick," Sophie told them.

Another Amish woman came out of the house with a pitcher of fruit punch and one of iced tea. Her gaze settled on Paul standing behind Clara. "Go away, Paul. We women want to talk about the men and we can't do that if you are standing here."

Paul swept one hand toward her. "This is Fannie Bowman. If you couldn't guess, she is the wife of another cousin. Noah Bowman."

"It's good to meet you, Clara. I've heard a

lot about you and your children. Now scram, Paul. Men are not welcome until we are done gossiping."

"That includes you, Nick," Anna said.

Nick heaved his tall frame out of the folding lawn chair. "Come on, Paul. Let's see if we can get in the horseshoe game. I've been waiting to settle the score with you since Hannah's birthday."

"Where is Hannah?" Miriam asked.

"Noah has taken her and some of her friends riding. He promised to have them back before we cut the cake."

"Here come some more of our friends," Willa said. Clara turned to see Debra Merrick and another woman approaching.

"Clara and Sophie, how nice to see you again," Debra said. "Let me introduce Janice Willard, the midwife who delivered Glen and Nicky, Rebecca's Benjamin and many other babies in our community."

Two nurses were soon peppering Clara with questions about Sophie's illness, her treatments and the planned liver transplant. Clara could tell that they were genuinely interested in her daughter's well-being.

"I am still researching how to make a filtered light tent. I had hoped to have the information for you today but there isn't a lot of literature on the subject. I still haven't found what type of plastic film is best."

"Are you talking about the window film that blocks UV light?" Helen asked.

"Yes." Debra looked hopeful. "Do you know anything about the different types of film?"

"I know a little," Helen admitted.

"Luke knows a lot more," his wife, Emma, said.

Helen nodded. "Mark and I purchased the film for our new display windows in the bakery from Luke's hardware store. Luke said it would reduce the amount of heat coming in during the summer and keep our furnishings from fading. Would you like to talk to him about it?"

Debra and Janice looked at each other. "Yes, we would," Janice declared.

"I'll get him," Emma said.

A few minutes later, Luke approached the group of women with an apprehensive look in his eyes. "I don't know what it was but I'm pretty sure I didn't do it."

They all laughed. Debra pulled a sketchbook from her bag. "We are investigating the use of UV-blocking film in the treatment of jaundiced infants."

"How can I help?"

Debra opened her sketchbook. "This is a tent

made of plastic film. Would you be able to obtain the materials to build something like this?"

He took the sketchpad from her. "Do you want the frame to be wooden or metal?"

"I'm not sure it matters."

"The cheapest would be a wooden frame. How big do you want it?"

Debra looked at Clara. "What do you think?"

"Six feet by six feet. Large enough to cover her sandbox." If Sophie had a place to play and to keep her occupied, she was more likely to remain outside in the light.

"Sure, I can order that for you but I thought you wanted something for babies?"

"I do," Janice said. "I have several pictures in my car if you would like to see what we have in mind."

The two of them walked away. Debra grinned at Clara. "It seems there aren't many problems that the Bowmans can't solve."

Clara caught sight of Paul watching her. "They are a remarkable family."

Before long, Sophie and the twins were busy playing with the puppets and with Clyde. Charlotte looked on with Juliet. As the women around her chatted happily, Clara was amazed at the number of people gathered for a one-year-old's birthday party and at the number of non-Amish people who had been welcomed.

It seemed that Bowmans Crossing was more than a group of houses near the bridge over the river. It appeared to be a gentle and welcoming community.

Miriam Bradley came over and sat beside Clara. "I understand you are facing some problems with your uncle's estate. Paul has told us about it. My husband, Nick, would like to ask you a few questions. Do you mind?"

It clicked in Clara's mind where she had heard the name before. "Your husband is the sheriff."

He and Paul came up behind her and settled in chairs on either side of her. "I am off duty today," Nick said. "Today, I am the proud grandpa of a darling little boy and nothing else."

Clara glared at Paul. "Is this why you invited me?"

"I did know that Nick would be here and I hoped that you would speak to him but that wasn't the reason I asked you to come. I invited you because I wanted you and your children to have an enjoyable afternoon. You have all been through a lot lately. I thought you deserved a little cake and ice cream."

"If you don't wish to speak to me, I understand," Nick said. "I would like to say that Ralph Hobson is well-known to my department. We have had many complaints about him in the past, mostly from the Amish. He takes advantage of their reluctance to report him. I would be interested in hearing what you have to say about him and this forged revocable trust and amendment he showed you."

Paul leaned forward with his elbows on his knees. "Clara, I believe you when you say your uncle would not leave the farm to Ralph. I'm asking you to trust Nick. He may be able to help you."

"In what way can he help me?"

"You said that your uncle used an attorney to draft the original trust."

Clara nodded. "I don't know his name."

Nick met Clara's gaze without flinching. "There are not many attorneys that work with Amish clients in this area. I can easily check to see which of them had your uncle as a client. If they have a copy of the original, it will be easy enough to compare signatures on the two documents. Let me do some checking for you. You don't have to file a complaint unless you want to."

Clara glanced to where her children were lining up to get a piece of cake. She wasn't doing it for herself; she was doing it for Sophie. She looked at Nick. "I don't want to file a complaint unless I have to but I can't stop you from asking questions."

"Fair enough. I don't want you to go against your beliefs. I see the riders returning." He rose and walked toward a half dozen young girls riding Haflinger ponies. The girl in the front waved to him and galloped up to him.

Charlotte came and sat in one of the empty chairs. "Have you made a decision, Clara?"

"About what?"

"Moving in with me. You said you would consider it."

"You truly want us to live with you?" Clara glanced at the women sitting around her. Was Charlotte being serious?

Charlotte's smile widened. "I think it is the perfect answer. I have plenty of room now that Helen and Mark have moved out. I liked having them here, I don't mean to imply otherwise but both Clyde and Juliet are ready for a change."

"I have two young, active children. Are you sure that won't be a problem?"

"Not as long as their young, active mother looks after them. If you are thinking I shall be worn out, perish the thought. Juliet and Clyde keep me every bit as busy as children would. Perhaps more so. Last summer, I had five grand-coons underfoot. They made for a difficult but rewarding time. Clyde, what's your opinion?"

The dog woofed twice.

Charlotte looked at the raccoon on her shoulder. "Juliet, do you have an objection? No? There you have it. Clyde has said it is an excellent idea and Juliet has no objections."

"It's very kind of you, Charlotte," Clara said, "but Sophie needs to sleep under special lights and that requires electricity. Would you object to a generator being used for that?"

"I have no idea. Clyde, do we object to electricity?"

Clara didn't know how she felt about having a dog make this major decision. Clyde tipped his head to the side as if considering the idea. Then he got up and loped toward the children playing by the edge of the river.

"Well, there you have it." Charlotte grinned.

The women all glanced at each other. Helen leaned over and laid a hand on Charlotte's arm. "We didn't hear Clyde's decision."

"Really? I thought he was perfectly clear."

"Just so there is no misunderstanding, what did he say?"

"He said he did not care for the noise and smell of a generator but it would be a small inconvenience and having the children stay at the house would more than make up for it."

"He said all that?"

Charlotte patted Helen's hand. "I have often said that you are a lovely person but you don't listen well. I know people say that about me but I hear everything. Clara, how soon do you think you and your children can move in? Of course, you will want to see the house first. Why don't we run over there? It's only two miles. I don't really mean that we should run. I would fall over in a dead faint before I reached the covered bridge. The horse could run but I always say never run your horse unless you absolutely have to. Getting them to stop could be a problem."

Anna rose to her feet. "I think the house tour should be delayed until after we sing 'Happy Birthday' to Nicky and everyone has had their cake and ice cream. Charlotte, will you help me serve?"

"Indeed, I will." She got up and followed Anna into the house.

Helen patted Clara's shoulder. "I hope my aunt didn't scare you off, Clara. She really is a wonderful woman even if she is a little bit scatterbrained sometimes. It would relieve my mind to know someone was living with her. The house is quite nice, plain and roomy. She has a lovely flower garden, too."

Anna and Charlotte came out with a stack of

plates and three tubs of ice cream. Anna called to the children, who came running for the treat. The men left their game and crowded around the table. After everyone sang to Nicky, he was allowed to grasp handfuls of his own cake and stuff them in his mouth. Charlotte began cutting the sheet cake while Anna topped each piece with the waiting child's preference of chocolate, strawberry or vanilla ice cream. The mothers in the group helped settle the youngest ones on the quilt while the cake and ice cream were being passed out.

Paul moved to stand beside Clara. "Are you enjoying yourself?"

"My head is spinning. I thought I was coming to let my children enjoy an afternoon of playing with new friends but it seems I have acquired new friends of my own, a place to live, a new treatment for Sophie's jaundice and I find the sheriff is willing to look into my cousin's dishonest dealing."

"So you are going to move in with Charlotte?"

"She has offered, and I'm hardly in a position to object. Apparently, Clyde is in favor of the idea, too. Juliet did not voice her opinion."

"That's great. Charlotte is a little odd but

she's a wonderful person. You could do a lot worse. Would you like to take a walk with me?"

The offhand tone of his voice belied the intensity in his eyes. She wanted to hear what he had to say. She wanted to get to know him better but was she risking a heartache?

Chapter Ten

Paul held his breath as he waited for Clara's answer. Surrounded by his family and the happiness they all seemed to share, he became aware of how empty his own life seemed. His brother and all of his cousins were working to secure the future for their children and the children of others. How many good marriages had he seen in comparison to the one unhappy marriage that he remembered? He wondered if Clara's marriage had been happy. Was she still in love with her husband?

"I would love to see the inside of the covered bridge if you don't mind showing it to me," she said at last.

He smiled with relief. "I'll be happy to give you the tour."

Together they walked to the far side of the

house and climbed up to the roadway. She paused. "Where does this road go?"

"The river makes a hairpin bend not far from here. There are farms, both Amish and *Englisch*, inside the bend. This bridge is the only way in or out. Actually, there is a place where a horse and buggy can cross the river if the water is low but it's seldom used. Our school sits inside the bend, as well. Timothy and Lillian both teach at the school."

"A man teaching school? A husband and wife both teaching? You have a very progressive congregation over here."

"I reckon that is true. We use a limited amount of solar energy. Some of our businesses use electricity from generators but no one is connected to the world by power lines."

She giggled. "I reckon you could say you are a wireless community."

He chuckled and started to relax. She didn't seem uneasy in his company, and that gave him the courage to continue their walk.

She glanced his way. "Tell me about your uncle's business."

"My uncle builds high-end furniture. It's sold in stores across several states. He has a business partner who is *Englisch*. He is the one who installed the computer for us and had a website built. He also pays for the upkeep of my uncle's website. It's a fine line we walk but our goal is to remain true to our Amish values and still provide employment for the young men and women in this area. Farming is becoming more difficult."

They entered the covered bridge. The sounds of the countryside became muted. He could hear the wind in the trees and the murmur of the water running under the bridge. It felt cozy and personal.

"I know how difficult farming has become for many Amish. My husband was unable to purchase farmland in our community. He ended up going to work for a carpet-manufacturing business. It wasn't ideal but it kept us fed. Eventually, he saved enough to start a part-time harness-making business."

"How did he die?" The Amish did not often talk about those that had passed on but he couldn't stem his curiosity about Clara's life and what made her who she was.

"It was an industrial accident. There was an explosion and fire at the factory. Three men were killed, including Lawrence."

"I'm sorry."

"*Danki*, it was God's will. I have learned to adjust because I had to."

"Why did you leave that community?"

She didn't seem to mind talking about herself. "Several reasons. There wasn't employment for me. My mother sold her house to help pay for Sophie's medical bills. She moved to Maryland with a friend. They are happy to be making quilts and exploring the beach. After Mamm left, I didn't feel connected to the people there. I knew Sophie would need more medical care. Our community was a poor one. They were unable to raise the money needed for Sophie's surgery. There were five children with severe genetic diseases in our church district alone. When my Uncle Eli wrote and invited me to stay with him, I was happy to come. I'm sure it must've been my mother's idea. Some people thought Eli was a grumpy old fellow but he was truly a kind man to me and my children. I'm happy I got to spend many of his last days with him. What about you? Did you grow up here?"

"*Nee*, like you, I am from Pennsylvania. My mother and stepfather still live there along with my five sisters." His words echoed back from the darkness overhead.

"Are you and Mark the only boys?"

"We call each other brother but we are not related. My father died when I was six. My mother married Mark's father a few years later."

"Do you remember your father? I often

wonder how much Toby will remember about his *daed*."

"I recall vague things. He wasn't a happy man. I don't think my parents had a good marriage. At least not according to him. I do remember he said we were like two peas in a pod." He stopped talking as an old memory surfaced. His mother scolding him for being just like his father. Never satisfied with what he had. Always looking for something better.

It wasn't that he was afraid to commit to a woman because she might not be what she seemed. He was the one who would never be satisfied.

Clara glanced at Paul from the corner of her eye. "What are your plans after the farm sale?"

They walked out into the sunshine on the other side. He drew a deep breath as he considered his answer. "I will pay back my brother and then the bank for the money I borrowed and invest the rest back into my business. Then I might sleep for a day or maybe go fishing."

"It has been ages since I've been fishing. You must go often with the river in your backyard."

He turned to the side and led the way to the narrow pedestrian walkway that ran the outside length of the bridge and started back across. It was easy to look over the railing and watch the water rolling beneath his feet.

"Not as often as I should. Why haven't you been fishing lately?"

"You'll laugh at me."

"I won't."

"I know you and you will. You are always looking for an excuse to laugh at me."

"That's not fair. I don't need an excuse to laugh with you, not at you. Tell me the reason you haven't been fishing."

"Forget I mentioned it."

"Now how can you say a thing like that? You know I can't let it go. I'll guess. You haven't been fishing because you hate to touch worms."

"Don't be silly. I don't mind worms."

He leaned back a little. "You don't have time because the children keep you too busy."

"They do keep me busy but that's not the reason."

"You haven't been fishing because you don't own a fishing license."

"I don't have a fishing license because I haven't been fishing. I don't see the point of paying for something I don't need."

"I've eliminated a lot of things. Is it because you don't own a fishing pole?"

"Now you're getting a little warmer."

"I know. You lost your bobber and you're afraid you'll never know if you have a fish on the line or not without it."

She chuckled. "Now you're very warm."

"Not a lost pole, not a lost bobber. I think I have to give up."

"I don't know how to put more line on my reel."

He sat forward to look at her more closely. "Are you serious?"

"Toby was playing with the rod and reel and he pulled all of the line out and it broke. I don't know how to put more line on it."

"It's a closed reel, right?"

"I guess. What other kinds are there? It has a compartment that the string goes into when you crank."

"You take hold of the front part and you unscrew the cap."

"It unscrews?"

He almost laughed at her shocked expression but he managed to keep a straight face. "*Ja*, the cap comes off and then you can see where to tie on the new string. Make sure you thread it through the hole in the cap before you tie it. Screw the cap back on and crank on your new line."

"Now I feel utterly foolish, and I give you permission to laugh at me."

He stopped walking and leaned on the railing to watch the water flowing underneath. "I don't want to laugh at you. I respect you too much for that."

"Now you're making me wonder where's the catch?"

"No catch. Can I ask you a personal question?"

She dropped a leaf into the water. "You can ask. I may not answer."

"Fair enough. Was your marriage happy?"

"I'm not sure how to judge happiness. Did I love my husband? I did. Was he a perfect man? He was not. He struggled with accepting Sophie's condition. Especially after we learned that more of our children could be born with the disease. He believed God was punishing him. Instead of embracing the marvelous gifts God had given us, he withdrew from the children. I don't think he meant to hurt them. I think he didn't want to be hurt when he lost them."

"It explains Toby's hero worship of me."

She chuckled. "I hoped that you hadn't noticed."

"He sometimes resents Sophie for the attention she gets from you, and he feels guilty about it."

"I don't know what I can do to change that."

"I'm sure you don't feel like taking advice on child rearing from someone who's never gone on more than three dates with anyone but I understand the need to have a parent's attention. Find something that you and he can do together."

"Like fishing?"

"That would be a wonderful starting place."

"How did you end up being an expert on children?"

"It's easy. I'm really just a big kid myself. My family will help you move to Charlotte's place whenever you want."

They started walking again and soon left the bridge. "I don't want to go but there is no reason to drag my feet. I will feel bad if you help me move and then must return all my things when it turns out that I do own the property."

He stopped to gaze at her. "We will all rejoice when that happens."

On Monday, at least half the people who had attended the party showed up to help Clara pack up and move to Charlotte's home. Her clothes, the children's clothes and Sophie's special canopy bed were all easy choices. The hard choices were the little things. Should she take the cookbook that had belonged to her grandmother or should it stay with the house? Her uncle's desk was hard to part with, as was the couch in the living room.

Clara sat down on the sofa and closed her eyes. "Are you all right?" Paul asked.

She looked over to see him watching her with the worried expression. She was the one who worried about everyone else. It was nice to have someone worry about her. "I'm fine."

"You don't look fine."

She ran her hands over the worn blue fabric. "This is where I read bible stories to my children every night. I have not lived here for that long but there are many good and tender memories here."

"Those you take with you. Ralph cannot sell memories. Have you heard from Opal Kauffman?"

"Only that her father is holding his own."

"He is still not able to communicate?"

"She says he is not. I can only pray that a few more weeks will make all the difference for him and for me."

"In the meantime, are there any of the books that belong to you?"

She smiled. "They all belong to me. Eli did not like reading except for his farm journals."

"Of course I would pick the heavy task."

"Never fear, I shall help you."

As they worked side by side, Clara was struck by how natural it felt. She was more at ease with Paul than with any man she could remember.

Charlotte was as excited as a small child on Christmas morning when Paul stopped the wagon in front of her house. She clapped her hands with delight. "I'm so glad you are here. I do hope you'll be happy with Juliet, Clyde and me."

"I'm sure I will be. Let us put Sophie's room together first since getting her lights set up and working are the priority." It turned out to be easy enough. Samuel and Paul had the bed moved in without any trouble while Luke worked on a stepladder to secure the hooks in the ceiling that would hold the light canopy. The long lights were unpacked and installed one by one. Isaac and Mark set up the generator on the back porch, where the fumes wouldn't be drawn into the house. When they started it, Clara held her breath as she flipped the switch and all the lights came on. A small cheer went around the room.

"Ooh, they are so pretty." Charlotte held her hands clasped beneath her chin.

Clara and Paul shared a speaking glance as they both struggled not to laugh out loud.

Paul's smile faded as his expression grew serious. Clara looked away first. She recognized the look of longing in his eyes, and she didn't know how to respond.

* * *

Two days later, Paul decided to see how Clara and the children were getting along with Charlotte. He had avoided seeing them sooner because he wanted to give them time to settle in and because he needed time to examine his changing feelings toward Clara. He was falling for the widow and her family but he wasn't ready to admit it out loud.

As he approached, he saw Clara wrestling with a large sheet of plastic film and something that looked like a frame for a greenhouse. He stepped down from his buggy. "What are you doing?"

"I'm building a playhouse for Sophie out of some lumber Charlotte had in a shed and this special plastic sheeting. It's a way to let the sun lower her bilirubin levels without giving her a sunburn."

"Interesting. Your carpentry skills are impressive. Where is Charlotte?"

"Baking cookies."

"Can I give you a hand?"

"I thought you would never ask."

He began to clap loudly.

She rolled her eyes. "Paul, help or go away."

"Okay." Paul took the roll of plastic film from

her. "Let's get Sophie's new playhouse finished. You are blessed to have me as a friend."

"I do know that. Your friendship has been an unexpected gift, and I cherish it and you."

"That's good to know. I didn't want you to think I was interested in...wow, this is more awkward than I thought it would be."

"In courting me?" she offered.

"Yeah."

"Paul, I am older than you are."

"A couple of years. That doesn't matter."

She arched an eyebrow. "You didn't let me finish. I am older than you are. I have a child with a serious illness to care for. I am not looking for a man to court me. That is the furthest thing from my mind. If I can somehow arrange the surgery and know that Sophie has a chance at a normal life, then maybe I will think about myself. Maybe. So you don't need to tippy-toe around me."

"I figured that you would understand."

Clara was grateful for his candor even as she struggled to hide her disappointment. Her attraction to him wasn't returned. That was a good thing. She needed a friend more than she needed a boyfriend.

"It can't go in the shade." Clara walked ahead of him to the backyard and surveyed the grounds. An old tree held a tire swing and four railroad ties formed the border for a sandbox. The children came running outside to greet him.

He looked at Sophie. "Where do you like to play?"

"I like the sandbox. Toby likes the swing."

"What do you think, Clara. Shall we put it over the sandbox?"

"If she is occupied, she will be more likely to remain outside in it."

"Over the sandbox it is."

It took them an hour to put the frame together. Stretching the plastic film over it was easier. When they were done, all of them stepped inside. Sophie immediately sat down in the sand and began to scoop it into a toy wagon. After about five minutes, Clara and Paul looked at each other. She said, "It's too hot in here."

"You're right. Shall we leave the ends open? Or should we leave the sides open?" He walked outside and studied the frame.

Clara joined him. "I say leave the ends open."

He cupped a hand over his chin. "I think keeping the sides open all the way around will provide better ventilation. Plus, we can cut a small opening in the roof to allow hot air to escape."

"As long as the unfiltered sun doesn't shine directly on her skin I think we will be okay."

"This spot is going to be in the shade until ten or eleven in the morning." He glanced at the sun and judged its position. "It will get hot fast."

"Maybe moving it to the other side of the house would work better. That way, it will get sun all morning and shade in the afternoon."

"I was going to attach it to the railroad ties so it wouldn't blow over."

"There's nothing preventing you from moving the railroad ties to the other side of the house."

He made a disgusted face. "Do you know how much these things weigh?"

"You have big horses. I'm sure they can move four railroad ties."

"Very well. I will move the ties and you can move the sand."

She placed her hands on her hips. "How am I going to move all this sand by myself?"

"You'll come up with something. You're pretty smart."

She chuckled. "I'm glad you have confidence in me. I sometimes wonder if people don't see me as a hopeless case."

"Not hopeless but you have room for improvement."

"Look who's talking."

He pressed a hand to his chest. "Me? I have

room for improvement? You are mistaken. I'm charming, I'm talented. I can sell the shirt off someone's back before he notices. Hey, bidder, bidder."

Sophie came out of the plastic playhouse to stand between them. Clara looked at her daughter. "Do you see that? There he goes again. Loving the sound of his own voice. He is a vain man and not Amish at all."

"Hey, bidder, bidder, bidder. Who'll give me a penny for this opinionated woman's opinion?"

"Opinionated?" Her voice rose in mock outrage. She struggled to ignore the laughter lurking in his eyes.

Sophie tugged on Clara's apron. She looked down to discover her daughter's eyes wide in her worried face. "Are you and Paul arguing?"

"*Nee*, little one. We aren't. We are only teasing each other."

"Are you sure?" Her tiny voice quivered as a tear trickled down her cheek.

Paul dropped to one knee. "Don't cry, *liebschen*. We aren't mad at each other."

"Mamm sounded mad."

Clara sank to her knees and pulled Sophie into her arms. "I was just playacting. You know how Toby pretends to be a pirate sometimes? I was playacting like that."

Paul laid a hand on Sophie's head and wobbled it back and forth. "No more frowning. You need to smile or I will think you are mad at me."

She hid her face against her mother's dress. "I'm not mad at you. I like you."

"Only because I let you sit on Gracie."

Sophie glanced at him from the corner of her eye. "Are you going to bring her over today? That would make me feel better."

He burst into laughter. "You are a wheedler."

"*Nee*, I'm a Fisher."

Clara scooped her up and stood. "You are a Fisher who knows how to wheedle."

"A talent I suspect she gets from her mother." Paul rose to his feet. "Let's put the playhouse here temporarily and move it when we can decide which area gets the best light."

Clara nodded. "I think that's a good idea." She put Sophie down and the girl went back to playing inside the tent.

He grinned. "I have them sometimes. Good ideas, that is. How is life with Charlotte?"

Clara chuckled. "She has been as charming and as accommodating as possible. We are all settling in."

"That's good to hear."

"What's the news on the auction?"

"Ralph is happy that you have moved out. No surprise there. I've started on the inside of the house, and I have most of the items sorted into bundles."

"I don't suppose that you uncovered some critical documents?"

"I wish I had. Have you heard anything from Nick?"

Clara shook her head. "It has only been a few days." She walked into the garden and sat on the wicker bench beneath the rose arbor. The last of the midsummer blooms were fading but they still scented the air with their rich perfume. "The time is slipping away so quickly. Every day my hope fades a little more. Why is God doing this to me?"

He sat down beside her. "Don't despair."

"It's hard to accept that Ralph has cheated my daughter out of her chance for a normal life." Clara covered her face with her hand. "I can't forgive that and it's wrong of me."

Paul hated to see her so upset. He laid a hand on her shoulder. She leaned her head over and pressed her cheek against his fingers. "I wish I could take it all away."

She managed a wry smile. "I wou

He bent to place a kiss on her f sighed and lifted her face to hi resist the temptation. He gently

She didn't pull away. He cupped her head and deepened the kiss, awestruck by the surge of tenderness that filled his soul.

Chapter Eleven

Clara turned her face away and Paul released her. She touched her mouth with her fingertips and drew a ragged breath. "You're going to tell me this shouldn't have happened."

"I thought about saying that but it would be a lie."

"It won't happen again."

"I'm not going to promise that, either."

She cast him a sidelong glance. "You're flirting with me."

"It's what I do."

She wanted to be angry with him but she couldn't. "Are you going to tell me that you have fallen madly in love with me?"

"Are you going to believe me if I do?"

"*Nee.* I think you decided to distract me from my self-pity."

He cocked his head to the side. "Did it work?"

"Are you ever serious?"

"I can't remember a time."

She smoothed the ribbons of her *kapp*. "*Danki*, my friend."

"For what?" He reached out and wound one ribbon around his finger.

"For reminding me that I am more than the mother of a sick child."

He tugged on her ribbon. "Yes, you are. Much, much more. Don't forget it."

"If I do, my dear friend will be here to remind me." She turned her head to the right. "We have a visitor."

Paul had to lean to see around her. Clyde sat looking up at them with a doggy grin on his face. He stood, woofed once and trotted away.

Clara looked at Paul. "I thought you said he liked to jump on people."

"Only people who aren't paying attention," Charlotte said as she came out the back door with a plate full of cookies. "You two are very attuned to one another. Oatmeal or peanut butter?"

Paul scooted away from Clara's side. She missed his warmth and the comfort his nearness gave her. "Nothing for me," she said.

Paul rose to his feet. "I love oatmeal cookies."

Charlotte smiled at him. "Among other things."

He took two from her plate. "I have to get

going. I won't be around for a few days. I have a lot to do."

As he hurried away, Clara had the impression that he was running away from her.

Charlotte sat and took a bite of an oatmeal cookie. "I think I may have left out the cinnamon. How long have you known that you're falling in love with him?"

Clara took a cookie and sampled it. "You forgot the nutmeg. About five minutes."

"I believe you're right. It is missing the nutmeg. What are you going to do about it?"

Clara leaned a shoulder against Charlotte. "You can't add the nutmeg after the cookie dough has been baked."

And she couldn't force Paul into anything more than a flirtatious friendship. She would have to be content with that. Somehow.

"I have got to do something more for her. I feel like I'm helping steal Sophie's chance for a normal life." Paul paced in his uncle's living room while his brother and several of his cousins sat around him. He couldn't get the kiss out of his mind, or the overwhelming need to go kiss her again. It was ridiculous, and he knew it but he didn't know how to fight it.

He was grateful she hadn't taken it seriously. If only he could be so flippant.

Samuel stood by the back door watching the children playing with Clyde. "You are right about the fact that you can't just cancel your contract with Hobson. He will simply get someone else to sell the farm for him."

"Then someone else would have to deal with their conscience." And lose sleep over it.

"It might make you feel better but it won't improve Sophie's chances of getting a transplant." Samuel left the back door and came to sit in one of the chairs by the fireplace.

"I know. That's why I asked all of you here. I need your help. What can I do? Timothy, there has to be a way to raise the money for her."

"Holding a fund-raiser is not a problem," Isaac said. "Setting up to raise half a million dollars will take time and a lot of work."

"I don't mind the hard work. I'll do whatever it takes."

"The annual county firefighters fair is on next week. They raise a lot of money for the volunteer fire department." Timothy sat opposite of Noah at the chess table.

"What of it?" Paul asked.

"If we could add Sophie's name to the fund-raiser and say we are splitting the funds, most folks would give to her cause as well and it will bring attention to her plight. A lot of people will already be coming to the fair. I'm sure they'll be willing to support two good causes."

"You could take up a collection at the auction," Noah suggested.

"That's an idea." At least one good thing would come out of the day. "Timothy, can I leave the details of the fund-raising to you?"

"Sure. Do you need help the day of the sale?"

"I do."

"Count on me," Samuel said.

"Me, too," Noah and Timothy said together.

"Thanks. I don't know what I would do without this family."

"When is the date again?" Noah asked.

"Three weeks from Saturday."

"Got it. Don't worry. We will see that little Sophie gets all the help she needs."

"When were you going to tell me about this?" Clara shook a newspaper in Paul's face before he'd had his first cup of coffee. Thankfully, no one else was in his uncle's kitchen.

He pulled away from her. "Tell you about what?"

"About this." She stabbed a finger at an article in the paper.

"You knew the sale was going to be advertised in the paper. You knew that from the beginning."

"I'm not talking about the sale. I'm talking about the date. This is next week."

Paul frowned and pulled the paper from her hand. "Let me see that."

He studied the farm sale announcement. It included all the things he had told the paper about the sale. They had the right farm. But the date was two weeks earlier than he had planned. "This isn't right. It's some kind of mix-up. They will have to print a retraction and include the right date."

She fisted her hands on her hips. "They had better print a retraction."

"Calm down. I'm going over to the shop and call them right now. We can't have people showing up two weeks ahead of time. I won't be ready."

"I'm coming with you."

"Let me handle this. I thought you trusted me by now."

"I do. I'm sorry I got so angry. Opal sent a note to say Dan is making a recovery but it's slow. He may not be able to tell me anything before the auction, especially if it's held early."

"There is no guarantee he can tell you anything about the trust even if he does recover enough to speak."

She seemed to deflate before Paul's eyes. "I know. But he is my only hope. I have talked to everyone else who knew my uncle and none of them can help me."

He reached out and took her hand. "Clara, you have to have faith that things will work out. Maybe not the way you thought they would."

"Call the paper right away and make them change the date to the original one we decided on. I need more time, Paul. Sophie won't be able to use the lights forever. She needs that surgery. I can accept it if God calls her home before He calls me but I couldn't live with myself if I hadn't done everything possible to give her a chance at life."

He squeezed her hand. "I know. I want her to have that chance, too. Never believe that I am against you."

"I'm sorry. I accused you without thinking. It was such a shock to see it in black-and-white."

"Let me go over to the workshop and straighten this out. It was a simple mistake, and I'm sure they will fix it. I've arranged for flyers to be put up in the shops and stores. I've ordered roadside signs made with the right date. You will have your extra two weeks. I wish I could give you more time."

"I know you do and I appreciate all you have done so far."

When she looked at him like that, with unshed tears glistening in her eyes, he couldn't resist pulling her into his arms to give her the comfort she desperately needed. She melted against him as though she couldn't stay upright without him.

"*Danki*, Paul Bowman. You are a dear friend."

He wanted to be more than her friend. He wanted to be the man who had the right to hold her every day but he wasn't the fellow she needed. She needed someone she could build a future with. He had nothing but an overpriced van, the ability to make people laugh and buy items they didn't really need.

She raised her face to look at him. "I don't know how I would've managed without your help."

It took every ounce of willpower that he possessed not to kiss her. "You would have managed just fine. I have never met a stronger woman or a more amazing mother. I am honored to be your friend."

She dropped her gaze and sighed gently. "You think too highly of me."

He forced himself to let her go as she stepped back. He didn't know his heart could ache so much or that his arms could feel so empty. "I'd better get going and call the paper so they have time to get the changes in for tomorrow."

He walked out the door and he didn't look back because he was afraid she would read the longing on his face. She needed a friend and he would be her friend no matter what it cost him.

Clara watched him until he was out of sight. She was a fool for throwing herself at Paul in such a wanton fashion. It had been a moment of weakness and nothing more. Not so long ago she would have heeded her common sense and kept her distance from him. Recently, her common sense had taken a back seat to her loneliness and the desire to be held. Not just by anyone but by Paul.

She had been warned that he wasn't the marrying type. She thought she wasn't, either. Her children demanded all her time and energy, she needed a way to support them, a way to keep a roof over their heads but the more she was around Paul, the more willing she was to share those burdens with him. He liked her children and they adored him. Simply being able to talk about her fears and her hopes helped to ease those very fears. And Paul was very easy to talk to.

She went back into the house. Twenty minutes later, she heard Paul come in. She braced herself to act normal and not seek his embrace again. One look at his face sent thoughts of furthering their relationship out the window. "What is it, Paul? What's wrong?"

"Ralph called the paper and had them change the date. He called the printer and told him to change the flyers, too. He also made sure that they wouldn't listen to me when I insisted the dates be changed back."

"How can he expect you to get everything done in such a short amount of time?"

"I don't know what he's thinking. Maybe he thinks I have been stalling because of you. Maybe he wants to hire a new auctioneer, and he's trying to make me quit. I won't know until I can speak to him."

"That's it then. The farm is going to be his."

"He will sell it without my help. As far as I'm concerned, this is a breach of contract on his part. I'm out. I should have been since the start. I can't profit while you suffer."

"Don't do it, Paul. Don't withdraw."

"I don't understand. I thought you hated the idea that I was working for him."

"Originally, I did. But I was being selfish. I know that you need the commission from the sale to get your business underway and to pay back your brother. I know all that is important to you."

"Being fair and just is more important to me. Mark will understand."

"I believe that but only one of us should end up a loser because of Ralph's scheme. You have put so much work into this already and you deserve to be paid. 'For the scripture saith, thou shalt not muzzle the ox that treadeth out the corn. And, the labourer is worthy of his reward.' Timothy 5:18. It was one of my uncle's favorite passages."

"I can't put a financial reward ahead of you and your children."

"You aren't. If Ralph has someone else take over, that person may not be as kind to me and the children as you have been. The best way to protect us is to stay employed by Ralph. I know you don't feel right doing so but I want you to handle the sale of this place. You know it's more than a plot of dirt and an old house. It was a home and a man's life's work. It's important to me that it be handled with respect."

"Clara, I can't."

"I want you to do it."

"I wish there was another way."

She cupped his face. "I wish there was, too, but I don't want you to lose what you have worked so hard for. If you quit now, Ralph wins more than the farm."

"If you feel strongly about it."

"I do. I honestly do." Maybe her reasons were more selfish than she let on. She did want him to prosper but she couldn't tell him that seeing him every day was the real reason behind her suggestion.

The outside door opened and Jessica came in. "I'm glad I caught you, Paul. There is a voice-mail message for you from Opal Kauffman. She says her father would like to see you."

Chapter Twelve

Clara kept a tight grip on Paul's hand as Jessica drove them to the hospital. She tried not to get her hopes up but this was what she had been waiting for. Dan Kauffman had been Eli's best friend. She couldn't imagine anyone else he would've trusted with his last wishes.

Jessica pulled into the parking lot and stopped. She turned around. "I'll wait here for you."

Paul opened the door and helped Clara out. Together they hurried into the hospital lobby and took the elevator to the rehabilitation floor. At the nurse's station, they were directed to Dan Kauffman's room. Opal was sitting in a chair at the foot of his bed. She rose when they came in. "I'm glad to see you got my message."

Clara advanced to the side of Dan's bed. She was shocked at the physical changes to the once strong and outspoken man. "Hello, Dan."

He opened his eyes and stared at her. He looked to his daughter. She smiled at him. "This is Eli's niece. This is Clara. You remember her, Dad."

Recognition dawned in his eyes. He motioned with his right hand. His daughter brought around a dry-erase board and marker. He wrote on the board and Opal held it up for Clara to read.

I miss Eli. He was a good friend.

Clara grasped his hand. "You were as dear to Eli as a brother."

He nodded. A tear welled in his eye and trickled down his cheek. Opal dabbed it away. "Clara has something she wants to ask you, Dad."

Clara squeezed his hand. "Eli gave an important document to you. It contained his final wishes. Can you tell me where it is?"

Dan shook his head back and forth. Clara tried again. "Try and remember where you put it. It was important, so I know you took care of it."

Dan continued to shake his head. He pulled his hand from Clara's grasp and reached for the marker and board. Opal held it still while he wrote. When he was finished, he pushed it toward Clara. She picked it up. *Never gave me anything.*

Her heart sank. "Are you sure? It would've just been a couple sheets of paper. You might not think they were important unless you knew what they were."

He shook his head and wrote on the board again. This time, he wrote *Nothing*.

Clara struggled to hide her disappointment. She patted Dan's hand. "Thank you. You get well right quick. I'm praying for you."

He shrugged. Clara surmised that he didn't expect a full recovery. She thanked Opal and then walked out into the hall with Paul. He said, "Now what?"

"Unless the sheriff comes up with something, we are going to let Ralph sell the farm."

"Why don't we call and see if he has come up with any information?"

To Clara's dismay, Nick Bradley had been unable to turn up anything new on Ralph. Ralph's attorney was blocking their moves. He had located Eli's attorney but the man did not possess a copy of Eli's original trust. Eli held the only copy.

She hung up the phone and turned to Paul. "That's it. It's over."

Clara sat in Charlotte's kitchen with Charlotte, Anna and Helen. Charlotte was busy sweeping the floor.

Clara's heart was almost too heavy for words. "That is the end of it. No one knows who my uncle was talking about. Dan Kauffman was my last hope, and he says Eli did not give the documents to him. Ralph owns the farm, and I can't afford Sophie's surgery." Clara squeezed her eyes shut to stem the flow of tears.

"Do not despair," Anna said. "Your church will help pay for her medical care."

"We are a small congregation. I can't ask them to carry such a burden."

"So you are too proud to ask for help?" Charlotte continued with her sweeping.

"My pride has nothing to do with this. The surgery will cost many hundreds of thousands of dollars. We are a poor community. How can I ask this for my child when others may go without shoes for their children?"

"That's pride," Charlotte said flatly as she opened the door and swept the dust outside.

"How so?" Clara demanded.

Charlotte turned around with one hand on her hip. She shook the broom handle at Clara. "Because you believe you are the only one who should bear this unbearable burden. We are commanded by God to care for one another. You would take away another's chance to do as the Lord bids because you do not think it is fair to ask. Are you the judge of right and wrong in the world?"

"You know I am not." Charlotte's word bit into Clara's self-pity.

"When a man has only two loaves of bread in his house, and he gives one to a person in need, is he not more pleasing in the eyes of the Lord than a person who has many loaves and gives only one? If you believe you cannot ask your fellow Christians to comfort the sick, to care for widows and orphans or provide a child with lifesaving surgery because they are too poor, are you not saying that your judgment is greater than God's? I would call that pride." Charlotte turned to the refrigerator. "Are there any cinnamon rolls left? I believe Juliet would like to sample one."

Anna and Helen exchanged smiles. Helen pulled a plastic bag down off the refrigerator. "Juliet is welcome to sample these."

"*Danki*. Is your mother coming to the sale? Juliet and Clyde would like to meet her. As would I."

"I told her not to come. I think it would be too upsetting for her."

"You make up the minds of a lot of people, don't you?" Charlotte took the bag of rolls and went outside.

Anna smiled at Clara. "Charlotte has a

unique way of looking at the world but in one thing she is right. You should not take away the chance for people to do something good for others because you think they are too poor. Those that can give will give. Those that cannot may find other ways to aid you. Stop trying to carry this burden alone. It will take longer but we will raise the money you and Sophie need."

"If only I can be sure she will have that extra time."

"You will speak to Bishop Barkman about joining us in our plans for fund-raising?" Helen asked.

"I will," Clara answered.

Charlotte came back inside. "Juliet took it down to the river to wash and it fell apart in her hands. The look she gave me was quite a scold. Have you offered your cousin your forgiveness, Clara?"

"I have not," Clara said bitterly. "I know that is wrong with me but I can't forgive him for making my baby suffer."

"That is very small-minded of you, and not very Amish. Jesus forgave the men who nailed him to the cross. Anna, are there some grapes that Juliet might enjoy? They don't fall apart in the water when she washes them."

"You will find some on the bottom shelf in the refrigerator. I hope she likes the red ones."

"I don't know. I will have to ask her. Holding bitterness in your heart is a lot like filling it with hot tar, Clara. It spreads easily but it is very hard to remove and nothing good can grow where it exists." Charlotte took a few grapes and went out the door again.

Clara shook her head, amazed at Charlotte's ability to make her point in the most roundabout fashion. "I'd like to go back to Eli's house one last time. Helen, can you watch the children?"

"Of course."

When Clara entered her uncle's house later that afternoon, she found Paul sitting in the living room. A single lamp glowed on the table beside him. He had her family bible on his lap. "What are you doing here, Paul?"

"Finishing up some last-minute details. I'm wondering who I can ask to buy your bible cabinet for you. I'll be happy to reimburse them. It shouldn't be separated from your family or from this bible."

She sat down in the chair beside him. "Having the bible is enough."

"Do you know these verses by heart?" he asked as he ran his fingers over the carvings.

She looked at the beautifully crafted cabinet. "Some of them."

"They must have meant something special to the man who carved out those letters. I wish I knew who he was."

"He must've been a man of faith."

"Genesis 1:1," Paul said.

"'In the beginning God created the heaven and the earth,'—I know that one." She also knew Paul was feeling low on her account. She wanted to see him smile.

"The next panel on the front says Isaiah 26:3."

She shook her head. "I'm not sure of that one. Will you look it up for me?"

He thumbed his way through the book until he found what he was looking for. "'Thou wilt keep him in perfect peace, whose mind is stayed on thee—because he trusteth in thee.'"

Clara tried to absorb the words. "It's hard sometimes to keep our minds on Him when there is so much going on in our lives."

Paul nodded. "I need to work on that, too. The left side is inscribed with John 3:16."

"That is one we all keep in our hearts. 'For God so loved the world, that he gave his only begotten Son, that whosoever believeth in him should not perish, but have everlasting life.'"

"Matthew 5:44." Paul spoke so softly she had trouble hearing him.

"I don't believe I can quote that one." She waited until he found the proper page.

"'But I say unto you, Love your enemies, bless them that curse you, do good to them that hate you, and pray for them which despitefully use you, and persecute you.' Makes a man wonder if the craftsman knew Ralph would fulfill that description."

"This one I have not lived up to," she said quietly. "I have not blessed him, I have not done good to him nor have I prayed for him. Perhaps all this trial is God's way of pointing out the error of my ways. I'm ashamed to admit that I have been a poor Christian. I have not held true to my promise to forgive others."

"Philippians 4:13."

She knew that one. "'I can do all things through Christ which strengtheneth me.' You would think the bible was talking about Sophie's illness but I think this one is meant for me. It will take more strength than I have without God's help to forgive Ralph."

She read the next one off the cabinet. "Proverbs 22:6."

Paul smiled. "My aunt's favorite. 'Train up a child in the way he should go, and when he is old, he will not depart from it.' Daniel 6:22," he said.

Her gaze snapped to Paul's face. "Daniel?

Oh, Paul, you don't think that's what Eli meant?" Clara moved to the edge of her seat.

"Why didn't we think of this before?" He quickly found the book of Daniel and leafed through it. Nothing. He held the book up and shook it. No loose papers fell out.

Clara sank back in her chair. "Read what it says."

"'My God hath sent his angel, and hath shut the lions' mouths, that they have not hurt me—forasmuch as before him innocency was found in me, and also before thee, O king, have I done no hurt.'"

"I want to believe that I haven't hurt anyone but how can I ever be sure?" she asked, looking at Paul.

"The bishop says only God is perfect. We are not—but we must strive to be. He says we are not judged on our success, only on the efforts we make."

"What is the last scripture?"

"Romans 12:2."

"'And be not conformed to this world—but be ye transformed by the renewing of your mind, that ye may prove what is that good, and acceptable, and perfect will of God.'" He closed the book. "I should get going. It's going to be a long day tomorrow."

"I hope you know none of this is your fault."

"Knowing it and feeling it are two different emotions." He rose, placed the bible in the cabinet and lowered the lid. "Don't forget to take it out before the bidding starts."

"I won't." They walked together to the front door and out onto the porch. Clara gazed at Paul, wishing he would offer her the comfort of his arms. She knew the longing must be written on her face. If it was, he chose to ignore it, and he walked away.

Chapter Thirteen

The morning of the auction, Clara saw Paul's entire family pitch in to help him. Two of his cousins, wearing vests with yellow stripes, began directing traffic into the farm. Buggies, pickups and automobiles soon lined the lane and spilled over into fields beside it. Clara couldn't imagine so many people would be interested in her uncle's machinery and household items. More members of the Bowman family carried out beds, tables and chairs. Her family's beautiful bible cabinet was carried out last. The sight of it sitting on the grass was the last straw for her. She couldn't stop the tears that ran down her cheeks.

Toby grabbed her hand. "Don't cry."

"I can't help it. I know they are only things with no true value but they are things I wanted you and Sophie to have. They are part of the history of our family."

"Don't worry." Paul spoke from behind her. She didn't turn around. She didn't want him to see her this upset.

"I'm okay." Her voice quavered and she knew she hadn't fooled him.

He laid a hand on her shoulder. "I have asked my uncle to purchase the bible cabinet for you to keep. It's my way of apologizing for this."

She turned around then. "I was going to bid on it but I doubt I have enough money to purchase it."

"It will belong to you and your children once again. It will be the last item for sale."

"*Danki*, Paul."

"I wanted to do something."

"None of this was your fault. I don't blame you for doing your job. I hope my uncle's things bring a fine price so that you can collect a good commission. You have earned it."

"Not yet I haven't. I'll get started in ten more minutes. I would give anything not to have to go through this. Are you sure you want to stay and watch?"

She heard the pain in his voice and knew how badly he felt. His hands still rested on her shoulder. She tipped her head to press her cheek against his fingers. "'Not my will, oh, Lord, but Your will be done.' I want to stay. I want to hear this speaker system you value so highly. I want to see if you are as good an auctioneer as you claim to be."

"I have never met a stronger woman than you are, Clara Fisher."

She managed to smile at him. "Clearly, you have been associating with the wrong kind of women, because I am nothing special."

"I happen to disagree with that statement. We can argue about it later. I have to go." He left her and made his way through the crowd to his van, which had been set up in front of the barn.

Toby jerked on her arm and pointed. "Mamm, I see Grossmammi."

Clara looked in the direction he indicated. Her mother was walking up the drive with her friend Stella. With a glad cry, Clara rushed to embrace them. "What are you doing here? How did you get here? I'm so glad to see you. Why didn't you tell me you were coming?"

Her mother laughed softly. "One question at a time." She gestured to two Amish men standing behind Stella. "I'd like you to meet Alvin and Orrin Mast. They arranged for a driver to bring us here. I couldn't let my brother's belongings go into the hands of strangers without being here to support you. I know how much his gift meant to you and I know how bitterly we all regret that it has been stolen from us. We will raise the funds for Sophie's surgery some other way. Now where is my little girl? And who is this big strong boy beside you?"

"I'm Toby, Grossmammi. Don't you remember me?"

"Toby? Why, you have grown a foot since the last time I saw you."

"I can't believe you are here. Would you like some coffee and rolls?" Clara asked. "Paul's family is providing the refreshments."

"We stopped on the road for breakfast," Stella said. "I'm sorry Ralph has stolen your property. We must pray all the harder that he sees the error of his ways and repents before he is called to meet his maker. Is he here? Perhaps if I spoke to him."

"I saw him arrive a few minutes ago. I knew he would be here to collect his money before the day is over."

"I know this is disappointing but you must not let bitterness take root in your heart. I'm sure that Eli intended to provide for you and the children."

"I am sure, too. But we were never able to locate the document. Eli said in his last letter that he had given it to Daniel for safekeeping but Dan Kauffman knew nothing about it."

Her mother's eyes widened. "He said he gave it to Daniel for safekeeping?"

"Ja."

"Was that in the letter I forwarded to you?"

"It was."

"No wonder Eli didn't explain what he meant. He thought you would still be with me when you read it." A slow smile appeared on her mother's face. "Toby, run and tell the auctioneer to delay starting the sale."

The boy took off. Clara stared at her mother. "Do you know the Daniel he meant?"

"I believe I do. Where is Ralph? I'd like to speak to him."

Clara looked over the crowd. Ralph stood beside Paul's trailer. Toby opened the back door and climbed inside. Ralph must've heard what the boy said because he turned a fierce scowl in Clara's direction. She motioned for him to come over. He tromped toward them, looking angrier than she had ever seen him. Paul and Toby followed him.

"What is the meaning of this delay?" Ralph demanded.

"Hello, Ralph." Clara's mother looked him up and down. "You have created a great deal of trouble for your cousin and her children. You should be ashamed of yourself. What would your mother say if she were alive to see this?"

"I'm not causing trouble for anyone. Eli signed the farm over to me. Clara is the troublemaker. She brought the sheriff into this. The Amish don't invite the *Englisch* law into their business."

"But you are not Amish," Paul reminded him. He stood with his hand on Toby's shoulder.

Ralph rounded on him. "Get this auction started."

"Are you Paul Bowman?" Clara's mother asked.

He nodded once. "I am."

"My daughter has told me many good things about you." She glanced between Clara and Paul. "I can see for myself that she was right. Before the auction gets started, Ralph, I want you to know I forgive you."

Clara swallowed hard and closed her eyes. She had to mean it if she said the words. She waited for God's presence to fill her heart. "I forgive you, Ralph. I pray you will see the error of your ways and mend them."

"Fine. I'm forgiven." His voice wavered. Clara knew he had been affected by her and her mother's words.

Clara's mother turned to Paul. "There is one more place we must look for my brother's trust document."

Paul's eyes brightened. "You know where it is?"

"These are just stalling tactics," Ralph said. "I have the only valid copy."

Their conversation had attracted the attention of Paul's family. Sheriff Bradley made his way through the crowd and stopped beside Paul. "What's going on?"

Clara tried to hold back her growing excitement. She didn't want to be disappointed again. "Sheriff, this is my mother. She believes she knows who Eli gave the documents to."

Her mother smiled brightly. "Daniel isn't a person. It is a bible verse. Daniel 6." She walked over to the bible cabinet.

Paul's heart sank. "We have already looked through the bible. It isn't in there."

"Not in the bible. In the cabinet." Clara's mother pushed on the panel with the inscription and it slid open to reveal a hidden compartment. "My brother and I discovered it when we were little. We hid many things from our parents that we thought were valuable, like our comic books and a transistor radio. Our father heard us listening to the radio one night. The next morning, he asked us both where it was. Eli said with a straight face, 'I gave it to Daniel for safekeeping.' I almost gave him away by laughing."

The mine owner, Alan Calder, came up to

them with a fierce frown on his face. "I thought we were having an auction today, Bowman. Let's get started. I don't have all day to waste."

The sheriff ignored him and stepped up beside the cabinet. He glanced at Clara's mother. "May I?"

She nodded and moved back.

"What is going on here?" Calder demanded.

"We are getting to the truth." Nick bent to look inside and pulled out a tightly rolled-up sheet of paper and an envelope stuffed with cash.

"This is ridiculous," shouted Ralph. "You don't believe this last-minute charade, do you, Sheriff? This is just a stunt to delay the sale." He began backing away.

"Stay where you are, Mr. Hobson." The sheriff nodded to someone in the crowd and one of his deputies moved to block Ralph's retreat.

The sheriff then carefully unrolled the document. "This appears to be the original trust drafted by Eli along with a notarized amendment naming Clara Fisher as his beneficiary."

"It's a fake," Ralph said, looking wide-eyed and frantic.

The sheriff fixed his steely gaze on Ralph. "I happen to know the man who drafted the original document for Eli. He's here today. It will only take a few minutes to have him verify that this is the original. I strongly suspect the fake is in your possession, Mr. Hobson. You're looking at some very serious charges."

"You aren't going to pin this on me. It was their idea." He pointed to Calder. "Eli wouldn't sell the mineral rights. That's all he had to do— let them mine the coal under his farm ground. He would have made more money in a year than he ever made from growing corn."

"Shut up, Hobson," Calder muttered.

"Are you saying that the New Ohio Mining Company was directly involved?" Nick eyed the man.

Paul had suspected that Ralph was a coward behind his bullying exterior. There was fear in his eyes. "Yes. Calder came up with the whole plan. He knew the land was in a trust when he checked to see who owned it at the courthouse. He said all I had to do was claim Eli made me the new trustee and then lease the mineral rights to them."

Calder leveled his angry gaze at Sheriff Bradley. "If you have any questions for me, speak to my lawyer." He turned away.

Ralph caught his sleeve and stopped him. "I'm going to need your lawyer, too."

"I'm afraid that presents a conflict of interest for him. You'll get a public defender." He jerked away from Ralph and left.

"I don't understand," Clara said. "Why go to all this trouble? My uncle didn't have long to live. Why not wait and make the offer to me? I would have gladly sold the mineral rights."

Jeffrey Jones joined the group and tipped his hat to Clara and her mother. "Because they needed to be sure the new owner wouldn't start asking a lot of hard questions."

Paul started to see the picture. "The new fence on the east side of the property. It wasn't on the original boundary line. It had been moved to make it look like the mine owned more land."

The sheriff shook his head. "Seems like a lot of trouble just to hide a few extra acres."

"It wasn't the acres on top that they wanted to hide," Jeffrey said. "They discovered a large coal vein that travels due west of the main mine. They started mining it without checking to see if they held the mineral rights. Most of the mineral rights in this area were sold to the mining companies back at the turn of the century so they assumed they were within their rights. When they discovered their mistake, they had to take action."

"That's when they started pressuring my uncle about selling the property," Clara said.

Sheriff Bradley eyed Jeffrey closely. "Who are you exactly?"

"Jeffrey R. Jones." He handed over his identification and a letter. "I'm an investigative reporter. I've been looking into the New Ohio Mining Company for the last eighteen months and I have found a lot of dirt."

Ralph folded his arms over his chest. "I'm not saying another word without an attorney."

Jeffrey smiled. "Your attorney is going to make a ton of money off you, Ralph. I have had you under surveillance for quite some time, too. As a person of interest in several insurance scams in the past, I thought that's why you were here, to pull another scam. But when you wouldn't even hear my offer for the property, I knew you were onto something bigger."

Sheriff Bradley handed back Jeffrey's credentials. "If he wasn't pulling an insurance scam, what was he doing?"

"New Ohio Mining Company had been illegally taking coal out from under this farm for at least a year. If that had become known, the company would have had to pay millions in fines and legal fees. When Eli King wouldn't sell and then passed away, they still didn't know who owned the land. A little background checking would have shown them there were two contenders. An upright, law-abiding Amish woman and a less-than-upright swindler. They saw their chance to quietly get the mineral rights by making Ralph the new owner."

"I'm willing to testify against them if you cut me a deal," Ralph said. "They supplied the attorney, the notary and the forged document after Eli's death. No one knew Eli had amended the original trust until Clara told me."

Clara had moved closer to Paul. He took her hand in his. Her fingers were ice-cold. "I still don't see why Ralph needed to auction off the property. Why didn't he just sell it to them? No one would have been the wiser to the moved boundaries."

Jeffrey took his hat off and smoothed his hair. "Unfortunately, Ralph got greedy."

Paul remembered their first conversation. "They gave you a lowball offer."

"They thought I was stupid. They had a lot more to lose than I did."

Clara squeezed Paul's hand. "What does he mean?"

He gave her a comforting squeeze in return. "The mining company would have to buy the place no matter how high the bidding war went. Any other buyer would want a boundary survey done and the questions would start rolling in."

Ralph chuckled. "I thought they needed to sweat for underestimating me."

"Who was your accomplice?" the sheriff asked.

Jeffrey tipped his hat to Ralph. "I'm sure

he or she is long gone. It was a clever plan but you were toying with some really bad characters. You got off easy. Calder's company has popped up and folded a half dozen times under different names. Two people who opposed him went missing. It will be interesting to see how it all washes out in court. I expect a lot of finger pointing and that will make my story worth even more."

"Ralph Hobson, you are under arrest for forgery, fraud and attempted grand theft." Sheriff Bradley read Ralph his rights as he led him away.

Paul took both of Clara's hands in his. "As the rightful owner of Eli King's estate, what are your wishes?"

"I want you to hold a farm sale. I will match the commission offered by Ralph if that is agreeable to you."

"I accept your offer. When would you like me to hold the sale?"

"Would today be too soon?"

"I think today would be perfect. I'd better get started before the crowd gets restless."

Hours later, the western sky was aglow with beautiful orange and gold colors painted across a few clouds above the horizon. Paul and Clara both paused to take in the beauty after the crowds had gone home with their treasures.

Paul gestured toward the beautiful sky. "My sister-in-law, Helen, says, 'Peace is seeing a beautiful sunset and knowing who to thank.'"

Clara knew she couldn't let one more sunset fade into night without telling Paul what was in her heart. Life was too short and too unpredictable not to tell him what he had come to mean to her and her children.

"Paul Bowman, I love you," she said softly.

She felt him stiffen beside her. "You are just caught up in the joy of having things turn out as they did."

"That's true but it doesn't change the fact that I'm in love with you." She wanted to be held in his arms and feel the touch of his lips on hers.

He shoved his hands in his pockets and looked at the ground. He kicked a small stone and sent it flying. "Now you think I should declare my love, ask for your hand in marriage and we will live happily ever after, is that it?"

"I was hoping for something like that."

"I care for you, I do but I'm not the kind of man you need. With me, you'd be getting another kid."

She squeezed her hands together until her fingers ached. She may have made the biggest mistake of her life. "You are selling yourself short,

Mr. Auctioneer. I've seen how you are with my children. I've seen how happy you make them and how happy they make you. I think you are exactly the kind of man I need and want."

"Now see, that's where you're wrong. Your kids are wonderful. You're a beautiful and amazing woman but…"

When she realized what he couldn't say, her heart overflowed with love for him. "But? You were about to tell me you don't love me. You can't say it, can you?"

"Clara, I think you just like to argue. I can't give you the things you need. You know that."

"I don't. What is it that you think I need?"

"You need a serious and steadfast man as your helpmate. I'm not serious. No one would call me steadfast. You deserve far better, and as much as I admire you, I can't let you make this mistake."

She took his face between her hands. "Honestly, Paul. Why don't you just say what is in your heart? Stop denying it."

"I don't know what you mean."

She rose on her tiptoes and slipped her arms around his neck. "Say you love me." Then she kissed him.

It took every ounce of willpower Paul possessed not to gather Clara close and kiss her.

He loved her with all his heart and soul. He had nearly robbed her of her inheritance and her chance to see Sophie well and whole. It was only by God's grace that the truth came out.

Just when he thought he would break, she stepped back. He saw the confusion in her eyes and hated himself for causing it.

She didn't need a joker making her laugh. She needed a man who would believe in her completely, and not allow his own wants to blind him to her needs. Everything that led to the happy outcome for her today had been done by others. They were the ones who saved her, not him. "You deserve a better man than I am."

"I don't want a better man. I want you. Faults and all."

"You need to aim higher, Clara. Your children deserve better. Think of them. Find someone who isn't in love with the sound of his own voice. Find someone who loves you and you alone."

"I have, only he's too stubborn to admit that."

"I care about you, Clara, I do. And about your children, and that's why I have to stand aside."

He walked to his trailer, climbed in and turned his horses for home.

Clara ran after him. "You're not making this easy for me, Paul Bowman, but if you think I'm going to give you up because you didn't get to play the hero you are sadly mistaken!"

Two long, lonely weeks later, Paul stood on the banks of the river tossing pebbles in the water and watching the ripples spread out until they disappeared.

"That's a slow way to build a dam."

Paul turned to see his cousin Samuel walking toward him. Paul turned back to the water and tossed in one more stone. "It helps pass the time."

"Until when?" Samuel stopped at his side.

"Until I grow up and stop being a restless kid."

"I hope that never happens. I like you the way you are."

"I think I made a big mistake, Samuel. I don't know how to fix it."

Samuel reached down and picked up a handful of pebbles. He tossed one into the water. "I assume you are talking about Clara and her children? What kind of mistake did you make?"

"I think I fell in love with her. Worse yet, I let her fall in love with me."

"So you love each other. That's not a mistake, Paul. It is God working in your life for the good of you both."

"Now see, that's where you're wrong." Paul

heaved the last pebble as far out into the river as he could. "I'm not husband material. I'm sure not husband and father material rolled into one."

Samuel chose a flat rock and sent it skipping across the surface before it sank. "Exactly what is husband and father material?"

"You are. Joshua is. Luke is. You guys aren't insecure about taking care of a family. You know what to do and you do it. I don't have a clue where to start taking care of someone else. I can barely take care of me."

Samuel chuckled, causing Paul to frown at him. "What?"

"Paul, none of us had an idea of how to be a good husband and a good father. I pray for guidance every night and every morning. Raising a child is the most important task God has ever given me. Of course I am afraid I will make mistakes. But I trust in the Lord to guide me. As does Joshua and Luke. A man can't do the job alone."

"I guess I'm scared."

"As are a lot of men who stand in front of the bishop and promise to love, honor and cherish a woman for the rest of their lives but they stand there anyway."

"And if I fail at the most important task of my life?"

"Then you must pray that your spouse is

strong enough to help you get up and go forward again. Life is not stagnant. It's not a stone." Samuel tossed the pebbles in his hand into the river. "Life is like the water out there. It keeps moving forward. It flows around the stone. Build a dam and the water will stay still until it gets deep enough to flow over or around the dam and cut a new path. You have to ask yourself if Clara can be strong for you and if you can be strong for her."

"She's the strongest woman I have ever met."

"*Goot*, because I suspect you will be a challenging husband but a fine one in the end. When is her surgery?"

"Tomorrow morning."

"Then you should see about getting a driver to take you to Pittsburgh. I heard Abner Stutzman was looking for more work."

"Do you really think I can do it?"

"It doesn't matter what I think. What matters is that you and Clara love each other. Support each other and the rest of life will work itself out like water flowing around a stone."

Samuel began walking back to the house. Paul dropped his handful of pebbles, dusted his palms together and went to use the phone.

Early the next morning, Paul entered the hospital in Pittsburgh and learned that Clara and

Sophie were already in surgery. He chastised himself for failing her yet again. He wanted to tell her how much he loved her before she went into surgery but he was too late.

He was directed to a waiting room. As he entered the room, he saw Clara's mother, Betty, and her friend talking to a woman in blue scrubs. They all looked worried. A television played in the corner of the room but he paid no attention to it.

When the woman in scrubs left, Paul took a seat beside Betty. She smiled at him. "I'm so glad to see you, Paul. Thank you for coming."

"Have you heard anything?"

"The doctor who spoke to us said Sophie is doing great but they are having trouble keeping Clara's blood pressure stable."

Paul shivered against the chill that touched his soul. "She'll be okay, won't she?"

"We must pray for her and for the people caring for her. She is in God's hands. Sophie is doing fine and that is what Clara wanted more than anything. She is grateful to you, Paul, for earning enough money at the sale to pay for this surgery."

If all his efforts only led to her death, he wasn't sure he could live with that. He rose to his feet and paced the length of the room and back. "Where's Toby?"

"Bishop Barkman and his wife are looking after the boy until Clara comes home."

"It's good that the church is helping." He should have offered to watch Toby.

Paul crossed the room to look out the window. His last conversation with Clara played over and over in his mind. She had been right. He was in love with her but he had been too afraid of failing her to admit it.

A phone rang and the receptionist at the desk answered. After speaking softly with the caller, she put her hand over the receiver. "I have a call for anyone here with Clara Fisher."

Betty said, "You take it, Paul. I'm afraid I'll just start crying."

He took a deep breath. "Sure."

The receptionist gestured to a small cubicle. "I'll transfer the call over there where you can have some privacy. Just pick up the receiver when the red light comes on."

"*Danki.* Thank you."

He did as she instructed. When the red light came on, he picked up the handset. "This is Paul Bowman."

"Paul, I didn't know you were going to be there." It was Toby on the other end of the line.

Just the sound of the boy's voice lifted Paul's spirit. "How you doing, kid?"

"I'm fine. Velda Barkman makes great oatmeal-chocolate-chip cookies, and the bishop let me drive his buggy to the phone shack."

"All by yourself?"

"He came along just to watch. How is my *mamm*?"

"She and Sophie are still in surgery. I haven't seen her yet."

"I hope Sophie doesn't have yellow eyes anymore. Sometimes kids make fun of her and it hurts her feelings."

"I don't think they will make fun of her anymore."

"I wish I could be there, too."

He gripped the phone harder. "I know you do. I'll tell Sophie and your mother that when I see them."

"Okay."

"Toby, you are the *goot* brother. I love you, kid."

"Really?"

"Really and truly."

"*Danki*, Paul. Love you, too. The bishop says I have to get off the phone now. Bye." The boy hung up before Paul could say anything else. It was a good thing because he couldn't speak past the lump in his throat. He loved Clara's children and he loved her.

Please, Lord, give me a chance to tell her that.

Agonizingly long hours later, a young man

in blue scrubs came into the waiting room. "Is there anyone here for Clara Fisher?"

Paul and Betty rose quickly to their feet. The tired-looking doctor smiled at them. "Sophie and Clara are both doing fine. They have gone into the recovery room and you will be able to see them in an hour or so."

Betty pressed her hand to her chest. "That is wonderful news, thank you."

Paul's knees gave out and he dropped back into his chair. *She's doing fine.* They were the most beautiful words he had ever hoped to hear. He covered his face with his hands as tears of joy ran down his cheeks.

Clara struggled to open her eyes but her eyelids weighed a hundred pounds apiece. She couldn't lift them. A woman's voice said, "Wake up, Clara. There is someone here to see you."

"Are you sure she's doing okay?"

It was Paul's voice. How did he get here? Was she dreaming?

"She's doing much better now."

"Thank God for that." Clara heard the relief ripple through Paul's voice. Was he really here?

She tried harder to open her eyes and finally succeeded. His wonderful face swam into focus. She wanted to say hello but nothing came out of her mouth but a croaking sound.

"Try some of these ice chips," the nurse said as she placed a plastic spoon to Clara's lips.

Clara took the cold chunks, amazed at how wonderful they felt in her dry mouth. When they had melted away, she opened her eyes again.

Paul was bending over her. He laid a hand on her forehead and then moved to cup her cheek. "Hello, sleepyhead. It's about time you got up."

"How is Sophie?"

"She's fine," Paul assured her.

"She's right beside you." The nurse pointed and Clara turned her head to see her baby sleeping peacefully without the blue lights. *Thank You, dear Jesus.*

The nurse pumped up the blood-pressure cuff on Clara's arm. "You are in the recovery room. We'll be moving you to a room in the ICU in about an hour. On a scale of one to ten, ten being the worst pain you can imagine, how would you score the pain you are having now?"

Clara shifted in bed. "Five."

"I'll give you something to help with that."

"Will Sophie come to the ICU with me?"

"No, she is going to the pediatric ward. But we'll arrange for you to see each other often."

"Sleep," Paul said. "I'll be right here for both of you."

"See how well I know you already? I knew you couldn't stay away," Clara whispered. She smiled as she closed her eyes and drifted off to sleep without hearing his reply.

Sometime later, she heard Paul's voice again. He was speaking to Sophie. "And the baby bear said, 'Someone has been sleeping in my bed and there she is.'"

"I like this story," Sophie said. "I have yellow hair, too. Will it change colors now that I have part of Mamm's liver in me?"

"*Nee*, it will not change," Paul said, laying a hand on her head. "You will always be my Goldilocks."

Clara turned her head and found her mother close at hand. "May I have some more ice chips?"

"Certainly. I will tell your nurse." Her mother rose and walked away.

A few minutes later, a nurse came in with a plastic cup full of ice and a spoon. She glanced toward Paul. "Your husband is very good with your little girl. It's nice to see such an involved father."

Clara didn't correct her. She liked the idea that the woman mistook the Amish auctioneer for her husband. If only it was true.

The next time she opened her eyes, she saw she was in a different room. Paul sat beside her slumped in a chair. "I'm not the only sleepyhead," she muttered. He heard her and sat up, rubbing his eyes. She wished she wasn't so groggy.

"Can I get you anything?"

"A kiss would be nice," she thought and then realized she'd said it out loud.

"That's easy." He leaned in and placed a gentle kiss on her lips.

Astonished, she raised a hand to touch his face. "Why did you do that?"

"Because I love you."

She dozed off for a second or two but forced her eyes open. "What did I just say?"

"You said you needed a kiss. I gave you one."

"That's what I thought. Why are you here?"

He smiled softly. "Because you needed me to be here."

"I did. I'm very glad you came." She reached out her hand and he clasped it between his own.

"I will always be here for you and the children for as long as God will let me."

"What changed your mind?"

He smiled. "I can't live without you. I tried but I can't."

"How is Sophie?"

"She's doing fine. I took Toby in to visit with

her for a few minutes. He told her he would feed the cat for her until she got home. I sent your mother to lie down for a while. She has been sitting with Sophie but I could see she was getting tired."

"I can't keep my eyes open. I'm sorry. I need to tell you something. I need to tell you…something."

"They just gave you something for pain. Rest now and talk later. I'll be here."

"Danki."

"You're welcome, my love."

"I like that."

The next time Clara roused, she was in a different room. A nurse was taking her blood pressure. "I need to get your vital signs. What is your pain level?"

"I'm fine." She ached but she didn't want to sleep anymore. "Where am I?"

"In your room on the surgical floor."

"Can I go see my daughter?"

"The doctor wants you on bed rest for another twelve hours. Maybe she can come down here. I'll check with the pediatric floor."

Paul rose from a chair in the corner of the room when the nurse left and came to the bedside. "You look like you are feeling better."

"Maybe a little. I'll be better yet when I can see Sophie."

"She was sitting up eating Jell-O when I was there a half hour ago. Your mother is staying with her. You told me once that you loved me and I told you I wasn't the man you needed."

"I remember?"

"I was lying to myself. I love you, Clara Fisher, more than I thought it was possible to love another human being. And I love your children, too. I want us to be a new family."

She was afraid to hope that he meant it. "That would be the answer to my prayers."

"I love you. Please say you will marry me."

"Of all the ridiculous places to propose, this takes the cake, little brother." Mark walked in with Helen by his side.

"I think it's very romantic," Helen said.

Paul left Clara's side. "I don't have an answer yet so you will have to wait outside in the hall until I get one." He put his hand on his brother's chest.

Mark backed up. "Okay. Okay. Clara, put this fellow out of his misery." Paul closed the door in Mark's face.

"I will."

Paul spun around to face her. "You will put me out of my misery or you will marry me, which question did you answer?"

She smiled. "Both of them. Yes, I will put you out of your misery and yes, I will marry you. And yes, your brother is right—this was a terrible place to make a proposal."

"I will ask you again when we are on a quilt under the shade of a chestnut tree watching the children play by the river."

"That will be a much better place."

"Only if the answer is the same."

She smiled. "It will be. I'm never letting you off the hook."

"*Goot*, because I need a strong woman to keep me in line."

"And I need a funny husband who will make me laugh."

"We will make a good team, won't we?"

She nodded. "We will. I will ask for kisses and you will oblige me."

"Absolutely, starting right now." He bent over the hospital bed railing and brushed her lips gently with his own.

There was a knock at the door and it opened to reveal her mother pushing Sophie in a wheelchair. Her daughter's bright smile was exactly what Clara needed to see. A group of people crowded in behind her—all the Bowman brothers and their wives, Isaac and Anna, Mark and Helen, and even Charlotte came in pulling a large suitcase on wheels.

Paul dropped to his knees beside Sophie as Clara's mother pushed her up beside the bed.

Clara reached through the rails to squeeze her daughter's hand. "How are you?"

"I'm *goot*. My eyes aren't yellow anymore."

"I'm so glad." Tears of joy gathered in Clara's eyes. God was good indeed.

Paul took Sophie's other hand. "I have a question to ask you, Goldilocks. Can I marry your mother?"

"Does that mean I can ride Gracie whenever I want?"

"No, it does not. You can only ride her when I am with you."

Sophie gave a deep sigh. "Okay, you can marry Mamm. Will that make you my *daed*? Will I be a Bowman now?"

"*Ja*, I will be your *daed* and you will be a member of the Bowman family."

Sophie gave a quick nod. "I think I'll like that."

Charlotte clapped her hands. "Oh, Clyde was right again. I can't wait to tell him."

She unzipped her suitcase and Clyde stuck his head out. Charlotte grasped his face between her hands. "Did your big ears hear that? These two are going to get married, just as you predicted. You are such a smart dog."

The door opened behind the crowd. "I'm sorry, folks, but only four visitors at a time.

Some of you will have to leave now," an annoyed nurse said but Clara couldn't see her.

Charlotte pushed Clyde's head back in the suitcase and folded in his ears before zipping it shut. "We're leaving," she said as she made her way through the group. It wasn't until Clara saw the back of the suitcase that she noticed it was full of holes. Charlotte had discovered a way to sneak her beloved dog in after all.

"We'll see you later," Anna said and pulled Isaac toward the door. One by one the Bowmans all wished her well.

From her bed, Clara surveyed the people who had come to mean so much to her and her children. When they left, she gazed at Paul with all the love in her heart. "I'm going to enjoy being part of the Bowman family."

"Not as much as I will enjoy having you and the children as my family."

"Could I have another kiss?"

"Yes, my love, you may. All the kisses you want." He leaned over the bed rail and tenderly kissed her forehead and her cheeks, then settled on her lips. When he drew away he smiled at her. "I'm the most blessed man in the world."

* * * * *

*If you enjoyed this story,
look for the other books
in the* AMISH BACHELORS *series:*

*AN AMISH HARVEST
AN AMISH NOEL
HIS AMISH TEACHER
THEIR PRETEND AMISH COURTSHIP
AMISH CHRISTMAS TWINS
AN UNEXPECTED AMISH ROMANCE*

Dear Reader,

I was sorry to say goodbye to the folks of Bowmans Crossing. Each time I create a new community, it comes alive for me with houses and stores, people and pets, bridges and rivers. It's a joy to recreate in some simple way the glory that God has placed in front of our eyes every day.

I fell in love with Clyde. I must admit I'm a dog person. In a few years, I may be as devious and ditzy as Charlotte. She was way too much fun to write. She will remain one of my most endearing characters. I wish I had thought of her sooner. I could have used her in all six of the *Bachelor* books. Oh well.

Everyone who has been in love knows the path it leads us down isn't smooth. It can be a great trip or it can be a trial, but I am a firm believer that love prevails. I guess that's why I write romance books.

So what's next for me? I'm happy to say I'm off to create a new Amish community, where love always wins and kindness is the order of the day.

Blessings to all,

Patricia Davids

Get 4 FREE REWARDS!

We'll send you 2 FREE Books plus 2 FREE Mystery Gifts.

TEXAS RANGER SHOWDOWN

Margaret Daley

SECRET PAST

SHAREE STOVER

Love Inspired® Suspense books feature Christian characters facing challenges to their faith... and lives.

FREE Value Over $20

YES! Please send me 2 FREE Love Inspired® Suspense novels and my 2 FREE mystery gifts (gifts are worth about $10 retail). After receiving them, if I don't wish to receive any more books, I can return the shipping statement marked "cancel." If I don't cancel, I will receive 4 brand-new novels every month and be billed just $5.24 each for the regular-print edition or $5.74 each for the larger-print edition in the U.S., or $5.74 each for the regular-print edition or $6.24 each for the larger-print edition in Canada. That's a savings of at least 13% off the cover price. It's quite a bargain! Shipping and handling is just 50¢ per book in the U.S. and 75¢ per book in Canada*. I understand that accepting the 2 free books and gifts places me under no obligation to buy anything. I can always return a shipment and cancel at any time. The free books and gifts are mine to keep no matter what I decide.

Choose one: ☐ **Love Inspired® Suspense**
Regular-Print
(153/353 IDN GMY5)

☐ **Love Inspired® Suspense**
Larger-Print
(107/307 IDN GMY5)

Name (please print)

Address   Apt. #

City   State/Province   Zip/Postal Code

Mail to the **Reader Service:**
IN U.S.A.: P.O. Box 1341, Buffalo, NY 14240-8531
IN CANADA: P.O. Box 603, Fort Erie, Ontario L2A 5X3

Want to try two free books from another series! Call 1-800-873-8635 or visit www.ReaderService.com.

*Terms and prices subject to change without notice. Prices do not include applicable taxes. Sales tax applicable in N.Y. Canadian residents will be charged applicable taxes. Offer not valid in Quebec. This offer is limited to one order per household. Books received may not be as shown. Not valid for current subscribers to Love Inspired Suspense books. All orders subject to approval. Credit or debit balances in a customer's account(s) may be offset by any other outstanding balance owed by or to the customer. Please allow 4 to 6 weeks for delivery. Offer available while quantities last.

Your Privacy—The Reader Service is committed to protecting your privacy. Our Privacy Policy is available online at www.ReaderService.com or upon request from the Reader Service. We make a portion of our mailing list available to reputable third parties that offer products we believe may interest you. If you prefer that we not exchange your name with third parties, or if you wish to clarify or modify your communication preferences, please visit us at www.ReaderService.com/consumerschoice or write to us at Reader Service Preference Service, P.O. Box 9062, Buffalo, NY 14240-9062. Include your complete name and address.

LIS18

Get 4 FREE REWARDS!

We'll send you 2 FREE Books plus 2 FREE Mystery Gifts.

YES! Please send me 2 FREE Harlequin® Heartwarming™ Larger-Print novels and my 2 FREE mystery gifts (gifts worth about $10 retail). After receiving them, if I don't wish to receive any more books, I can return the shipping statement marked "cancel." If I don't cancel, I will receive 4 brand-new larger-print novels every month and be billed just $5.49 per book in the U.S. or $6.24 per book in Canada. That's a savings of at least 19% off the cover price. It's quite a bargain! Shipping and handling is just 50¢ per book in the U.S. and 75¢ per book in Canada*. I understand that accepting the 2 free books and gifts places me under no obligation to buy anything. I can always return a shipment and cancel at any time. The free books and gifts are mine to keep no matter what I decide.

161/361 IDN GMY3

Name (please print)

Address   Apt. #

City   State/Province   Zip/Postal Code

Mail to the **Reader Service:**
IN U.S.A.: P.O. Box 1341, Buffalo, NY 14240-8531
IN CANADA: P.O. Box 603, Fort Erie, Ontario L2A 5X3

Want to try two free books from another series? Call 1-800-873-8635 or visit www.ReaderService.com.

HW18

HOME on the RANCH

YES! Please send me the **Home on the Ranch Collection** in Larger Print. This collection begins with 3 FREE books and 2 FREE gifts in the first shipment. Along with my 3 free books, I'll also get the next 4 books from the Home on the Ranch Collection, in LARGER PRINT, which I may either return and owe nothing, or keep for the low price of $5.24 U.S./ $5.89 CDN each plus $2.99 for shipping and handling per shipment*. If I decide to continue, about once a month for 8 months I will get 6 or 7 more books, but will only need to pay for 4. That means 2 or 3 books in every shipment will be FREE! If I decide to keep the entire collection, I'll have paid for only 32 books because 19 books are FREE! I understand that accepting the 3 free books and gifts places me under no obligation to buy anything. I can always return a shipment and cancel at any time. My free books and gifts are mine to keep no matter what I decide.

268 HCN 3760 468 HCN 3760

Name	(PLEASE PRINT)
Address	Apt. #
City	State/Prov.	Zip/Postal Code

Signature (if under 18, a parent or guardian must sign)

Mail to the **Reader Service**:

IN U.S.A.: P.O. Box 1867, Buffalo, NY. 14240-1867
IN CANADA: P.O. Box 609, Fort Erie, Ontario L2A 5X3

* Terms and prices subject to change without notice. Prices do not include applicable taxes. Sales tax applicable in NY. Canadian residents will be charged applicable taxes. This offer is limited to one order per household. All orders subject to approval. Credit or debit balances in a customer's account(s) may be offset by any other outstanding balance owed by or to the customer. Please allow 3 to 4 weeks for delivery. Offer available while quantities last. Offer not available to Quebec residents.

READERSERVICE.COM

Manage your account online!

- Review your order history
- Manage your payments
- Update your address

*We've designed the
Reader Service website
just for you.*

Enjoy all the features!

- Discover new series available to you, and read excerpts from any series.
- Respond to mailings and special monthly offers.
- Browse the Bonus Bucks catalog and online-only exculsives.
- Share your feedback.